SPECIAL MESSAGE

THE ULVERSCROFT
(registered UK charity

was established in 1972 to provide funds for research, diagnosis and treatment of eye diseases. Examples of major projects funded by the Ulverscroft Foundation are:-

- The Children's Eye Unit at Moorfields Eye Hospital, London
- The Ulverscroft Children's Eye Unit at Great Ormond Street Hospital for Sick Children
- Funding research into eye diseases and treatment at the Department of Ophthalmology, University of Leicester
- The Ulverscroft Vision Research Group, Institute of Child Health
- Twin operating theatres at the Western Ophthalmic Hospital, London
- The Chair of Ophthalmology at the Royal Australian College of Ophthalmologists

You can help further the work of the Foundation by making a donation or leaving a legacy. Every contribution is gratefully received. If you would like to help support the Foundation or require further information, please contact:

THE ULVERSCROFT FOUNDATION
The Green, Bradgate Road, Anstey
Leicester LE7 7FU, England
Tel: (0116) 236 4325

website: www.foundation.ulverscroft.com

Sir Arthur Conan Doyle was born in Edinburgh, Scotland, in 1859. He studied medicine at the University of Edinburgh, where he met Dr. Joseph Bell, upon whose habits and abilities in the sphere of deductive reasoning Doyle would later base his most famous creation, Sherlock Holmes. After working for a time as a ship's doctor, he established his own medical practice near Portsmouth, where the lack of patients led to him spending his time working on his Holmesian stories — the enormous success of which later enabled him to give up the practice and devote his time to writing. During the Boer War, Doyle served as a volunteer doctor in the Langman Field Hospital, Bloemfontein. A fervent advocate of justice, he was also a campaigner for reform of the Congo Free State; domestically, he personally investigated two closed criminal cases, which led to both of the accused being exonerated of the crimes. A prolific author — whose works included science fiction, crime fiction, historical novels, poetry, and political treatises — he died in 1930.

THE GREAT SHADOW

When Jock Calder's orphaned cousin Edie
arrives to stay with his family, both he and
his friend Jim Horscroft quickly lose their
hearts to her. As the year turns, and the
Allies march into Paris, it seems the great
shadow of Napoleon will no longer
menace Europe. Then Bonaventure de
Lapp appears on the shore, claiming to be
the survivor of a shipwreck. The Calders
take him in — only to discover that Edie
has married him in secret. As Jock and Jim
reel from the revelation, further devastat-
ing news arrives — Napoleon has broken
free from his exile, and Jock and Jim must
march to the field of Waterloo . . .

SIR ARTHUR CONAN DOYLE

THE GREAT SHADOW

Complete and Unabridged

ULVERSCROFT
Leicester

First published in Great Britain in 1892

This Large Print Edition
published 2016

The moral right of the author has been asserted

A catalogue record for this book is available
from the British Library.

ISBN 978–1–4448–2939–6

Published by
F. A. Thorpe (Publishing)
Anstey, Leicestershire

Set by Words & Graphics Ltd.
Anstey, Leicestershire
Printed and bound in Great Britain by
T. J. International Ltd., Padstow, Cornwall

This book is printed on acid-free paper

Contents

1. The Night of the Beacons 1

2. Cousin Edie of Eyemouth 17

3. The Shadow on the Waters 29

4. The Choosing of Jim 42

5. The Man From the Sea 56

6. A Wandering Eagle......................69

7. The Corriemuir Peel Tower 78

8. The Coming of the Cutter 96

9. The Doings at West Inch..............102

10. The Return of the Shadow 108

11. The Gathering of the Nations........118

12. The Shadow on the Land.............132

13. The End of the Storm................154

14. The Tally of Death 164

15. The End of It 170

1

The Night of the Beacons

It is strange to me, Jock Calder of West Inch, to feel that though now, in the very centre of the nineteenth century, I am but five-and-fifty years of age, and though it is only once in a week perhaps that my wife can pluck out a little grey bristle from over my ear, yet I have lived in a time when the thoughts and the ways of men were as different as though it were another planet from this. For when I walk in my fields I can see, down Berwick way, the little fluffs of white smoke which tell me of this strange new hundred-legged beast, with coals for food and a thousand men in its belly, for ever crawling over the border. On a shiny day I can see the glint of the brass work as it takes the curve near Corriemuir; and then, as I look out to sea, there is the same beast again, or a dozen of them maybe, leaving a trail of black in the air and of white in the water, and swimming in the face of the wind as easily as a salmon up the Tweed. Such a sight as that would have struck my good old father speechless with wrath as well as surprise; for he was

1

so stricken with the fear of offending the Creator that he was chary of contradicting Nature, and always held the new thing to be nearly akin to the blasphemous. As long as God made the horse, and a man down Birmingham way the engine, my good old dad would have stuck by the saddle and the spurs.

But he would have been still more surprised had he seen the peace and kindliness which reigns now in the hearts of men, and the talk in the papers and at the meetings that there is to be no more war — save, of course, with blacks and such like. For when he died we had been fighting with scarce a break, save only during two short years, for very nearly a quarter of a century. Think of it, you who live so quietly and peacefully now! Babies who were born in the war grew to be bearded men with babies of their own, and still the war continued. Those who had served and fought in their stalwart prime grew stiff and bent, and yet the ships and the armies were struggling. It was no wonder that folk came at last to look upon it as the natural state, and thought how queer it must seem to be at peace. During that long time we fought the Dutch, we fought the Danes, we fought the Spanish, we fought the Turks, we fought the Americans, we fought the Monte-Videans, until it seemed that in this universal struggle no race was too near of kin, or too far away, to be drawn into the quarrel. But most of all it was the French whom we fought, and the man whom of all others we loathed and feared and admired was the great Captain who ruled them.

It was very well to draw pictures of him, and sing songs about him, and make as though he were an impostor; but I can tell you that the fear of that man hung like a black shadow over all Europe, and that there was a time when the glint of a fire at night upon the coast would set every woman upon her knees and every man gripping for his musket. He had always won: that was the terror of it. The Fates seemed to be behind him. And now we knew that he lay upon the northern coast with a hundred and fifty thousand veterans, and the boats for their passage. But it is an old story, how a third of the grown folk of our country took up arms, and how our little one-eyed, one-armed man crushed their fleet. There was still to be a land of free thinking and free speaking in Europe.

There was a great beacon ready on the hill by Tweedmouth, built up of logs and tar-barrels; and I can well remember how, night after night, I strained my eyes to see if it were ablaze. I was only eight at the time, but it is an age when one takes a grief to heart, and I felt as though the fate of the country hung in some fashion upon me and my vigilance. And then one night as I looked I suddenly saw a little flicker on the beacon hill — a single red tongue of flame in the darkness. I remember how I rubbed my eyes, and pinched myself, and rapped my knuckles against the stone window-sill, to make sure that I was indeed awake. And then the flame shot higher, and I saw the red quivering line upon the water between; and I dashed into the kitchen, screeching to my father that the French had crossed and the Tweedmouth light was aflame. He had been talking to Mr. Mitchell, the law student from Edinburgh; and I can see him now as he knocked his pipe out at the side of the fire, and looked at me from over the top of his horn spectacles.

'Are you sure, Jock?' says he.

'Sure as death!' I gasped.

He reached out his hand for the Bible upon the table, and opened it upon his knee as though he meant to read to us; but he shut it again in silence, and hurried out. We went too, the law student and I, and followed him down to the gate which opens out upon the highway. From there we could see the red light of the big beacon, and the glimmer of a smaller one to the north of us at Ayton. My mother came down with two plaids to keep the chill from us, and we all stood there until morning, speaking little to each other, and that little in a whisper. The road had more folk on it than ever passed along it at night before; for many of the yeomen up our way had enrolled themselves in the Berwick volunteer regiments, and were riding now as fast as hoof could carry them for the muster. Some had a stirrup cup or two before parting, and I cannot forget one who tore past on a huge white horse, brandishing a great rusty sword in the moonlight. They shouted to us as they passed that the North Berwick Law fire was blazing, and that it was thought that the alarm had come from Edinburgh Castle. There were a few who galloped the other way, couriers for Edinburgh, and the laird's son, and Master Clayton, the deputy sheriff, and such like. And among others there was one a fine built, heavy man on a roan horse, who pulled up at our gate and asked some question about the road. He took off his hat to ease himself, and I saw that he had a kindly long-drawn face, and a great high brow that shot away up into tufts of sandy hair.

'I doubt it's a false alarm,' said he. 'Maybe I'd ha' done well to bide where I was; but now I've come so far, I'll break my fast with the regiment.'

He clapped spurs to his horse, and away he went down the brae.

'I ken him weel,' said our student, nodding after him. 'He's a lawyer in Edinburgh, and a braw hand at the stringin' of verses. Wattie Scott is his name.'

None of us had heard of it then; but it was not long before it was the best known name in Scotland, and many a time we thought of how he speered his way of us on the night of the terror.

But early in the morning we had our minds set at ease. It was grey and cold, and my mother had gone up to the house to make a pot of tea for us, when there came a gig down the road with Dr. Horscroft of Ayton in it and his son Jim. The collar of the doctor's brown coat came over his ears, and he looked in a deadly black humour; for Jim, who was but fifteen years of age, had trooped off to Berwick at the first alarm with his father's new fowling piece. All night his dad had chased him, and now there he was, a prisoner, with the barrel of the stolen gun sticking out from behind the seat. He looked as sulky as his father, with his hands thrust into his side-pockets, his brows drawn down, and his lower lip thrusting out.

'It's all a lie!' shouted the doctor as he passed. 'There has been no landing, and all the fools in Scotland have been gadding about the roads for nothing.'

His son Jim snarled something up at him on this, and his father struck him a blow with his clenched fist on the side of his head, which sent the boy's chin forward upon his breast as though he had been stunned. My father shook his head, for he had a liking for Jim; but we all walked up to the house again, nodding and blinking, and hardly able to keep our eyes open now that we knew that all was safe, but with a thrill of joy at our hearts such as I have only matched once or twice in my lifetime.

Now all this has little enough to do with what I took my pen up to tell about; but when a man has a good memory and little skill, he cannot draw one thought from his mind without a dozen others trailing out behind it. And yet, now that I come to think of it, this had something to do with it after all; for Jim Horscroft had so deadly a quarrel with his father, that he was packed off to the Berwick Academy, and as my father had long wished me to go there, he took advantage of this chance to send me also.

But before I say a word about this school, I shall go back to where I should have begun, and give you a hint as to who I am; for it may be that these words of mine may be read by some folk beyond the border country who never heard of the Calders of West Inch.

It has a brave sound, West Inch, but it is not a fine estate with a braw house upon it, but only a great hard-bitten, wind-swept sheep run, fringing off into links along the sea-shore, where a frugal man might with hard work just pay his rent and have butter instead of treacle on Sundays. In the centre there is a grey-stoned slate-roofed house with a byre behind it, and '1703' scrawled in stonework over the lintel of the door. There for more than a hundred years our folk have lived, until, for all their poverty, they came to take a good place among the people; for in the country parts the old yeoman is often better thought of than the new laird.

There was one queer thing about the house of West Inch. It has been reckoned by engineers and other knowing folk that the boundary line between the two countries ran right through the middle of it, splitting our second-best bedroom into an English half and a Scotch half. Now the cot in which I always slept was so placed that my head was to the north of the line and my feet to the south of it. My friends say that if I had chanced to lie the other way my hair might not have been so sandy, nor my mind of so solemn a cast. This I know, that more than once in my life, when my Scotch head could see no way out of a danger, my good thick English legs have come to my help, and carried me clear away. But at school I never heard the end of this, for they would call me 'Half-and-half' and 'The Great Britain,' and sometimes 'Union Jack.' When there was a battle between the Scotch and English boys, one side would kick my shins and the other cuff my ears, and then they would both stop and laugh as though it were something funny.

At first I was very miserable at the Berwick Academy. Birtwhistle was the first master, and Adams the second, and I had no love for either of them. I was shy and backward by nature, and slow at making a friend either among masters or boys. It was nine miles as the crow flies, and eleven and a half by road, from Berwick to West Inch, and my heart grew heavy at the weary distance that separated me from my mother; for, mark you, a lad of that age pretends that he has no need of his mother's caresses, but ah, how sad he is when he is taken at his word! At last I could stand it no longer, and I determined to run away from the school and make my way home as fast as I might. At the very last moment, however, I had the good fortune to win the praise and admiration of every one, from the headmaster downwards, and to find my school life made very pleasant and easy to me. And all this came of my falling by accident out of a second-floor window.

This was how it happened. One evening I had been kicked by Ned Barton, who was the bully of the school; and this injury coming on the top of all my other grievances, caused my little cup to overflow. I vowed that night, as I buried my tear-stained face beneath the blankets, that the next morning would either find me at West Inch or well on the way to it. Our dormitory was on the second floor, but I was a famous climber, and had a fine head for heights. I used to think little, young as I was, of swinging myself with a rope round my thigh off the West Inch gable, and that stood three-and-fifty feet above the ground. There was not much fear then but that I could make my way out of Birtwhistle's dormitory. I waited a weary while until the coughing and tossing had died away, and there was no sound of wakefulness from the long line of wooden cots; then I very softly rose, slipped on my clothes, took my shoes in my hand, and walked tiptoe to the window. I opened the casement and looked out. Underneath me lay the garden, and close by my hand was the stout branch of a pear tree. An active lad could ask no better ladder. Once in the garden I had but a five-foot wall to get over, and then there was nothing but distance between me and home. I took a firm grip of a branch with one hand, placed my knee upon another one, and was about to swing myself out of the window, when in a moment I was as silent and as still as though I had been turned to stone.

There was a face looking at me from over the coping of the wall. A chill of fear struck to my heart at its whiteness and its stillness. The moon shimmered upon it, and the eyeballs moved slowly from side to side, though I was hid from them behind the screen of the pear tree. Then in a jerky fashion this white face ascended, until the neck, shoulders, waist, and knees of a man became visible. He sat himself down on the top of the wall, and with a great heave he pulled up after him a boy about my own size, who caught his breath from time to time as though to choke down a sob. The man gave him a shake, with a few rough whispered words, and then the two dropped together down into the garden. I was still standing balanced with one foot upon the bough and one upon the casement, not daring to budge for fear of attracting their attention, for I could hear them moving stealthily about in the long shadow of the house. Suddenly, from immediately beneath my feet, I heard a low grating noise and the sharp tinkle of falling glass.

'That's done it,' said the man's eager whisper. 'There is room for you.'

'But the edge is all jagged!' cried the other in a weak quaver.

The fellow burst out into an oath that made my skin pringle.

'In with you, you cub,' he snarled, 'or — '

I could not see what he did, but there was a short, quick gasp of pain.

'I'll go! I'll go!' cried the little lad.

But I heard no more, for my head suddenly swam, my heel shot off the branch, I gave a dreadful yell, and came down, with my ninety-five pounds of weight, right upon the bent back of the burglar. If you ask me, I can only say that to this day I am not quite certain whether it was an accident or whether I designed it. It may be that while I was thinking of doing it Chance settled the matter for me. The fellow was stooping with his head forward thrusting the boy through a tiny window, when I came down upon him just where the neck joins the spine. He gave a kind of whistling cry, dropped upon his face, and rolled three times over, drumming on the grass with his heels. His little companion flashed off in the moonlight, and was over the wall in a trice. As for me, I sat yelling at the pitch of my lungs and nursing one of my legs, which felt as if a red-hot ring were welded round it.

It was not long, as may be imagined, before the whole household, from the headmaster to the stable boy, were out in the garden with lamps and lanterns. The matter was soon cleared: the man carried off upon a shutter, and I borne in much state and solemnity to a special bedroom, where the small bone of my leg was set by Surgeon Purdie, the younger of the two brothers of that name. As to the robber, it was found that his legs were palsied, and the doctors were of two minds as to whether he would recover the use of them or no; but the Law never gave them a chance of settling the matter, for he was hanged after Carlisle assizes, some six weeks later. It was proved that he was the most desperate rogue in the North of England, for he had done three murders at the least, and there were charges enough against him upon the sheet to have hanged him ten times over.

Well now, I could not pass over my boyhood without telling you about this, which was the most important thing that happened to me. But I will go off upon no more side tracks; for when I think of all that is coming, I can see very well that I shall have more than enough to do before I have finished. For when a man has only his own little private tale to tell, it often takes him all his time; but when he gets mixed up in such great matters as I shall have to speak about, then it is hard on him, if he has not been brought up to it, to get it all set down to his liking. But my memory is as good as ever, thank God, and I shall try to get it all straight before I finish.

It was this business of the burglar that first made a friendship between Jim Horscroft, the doctor's son, and me. He was cock boy of the school from the day he came; for within the hour he had thrown Barton, who had been cock before him, right through the big blackboard in the class-room. Jim always ran to muscle and bone, and even then he was square and tall, short of speech and long in the arm, much given to lounging with his broad back against walls, and his hands deep in his breeches pockets. I can even recall that he had a trick of keeping a straw in the corner of his mouth, just where he used afterwards to hold his pipe. Jim was always the same for good and for bad since first I knew him.

Heavens, how we all looked up to him! We were but young savages, and had a savage's respect for power. There was Tom Carndale of Appleby, who could write alcaics as well as mere pentameters and hexameters, yet nobody would give a snap for Tom; and there was Willie Earnshaw, who had every date, from the killing of Abel, on the tip of his tongue, so that the masters themselves would turn to him if they were in doubt, yet he was but a narrow-chested lad, over long for his breadth; and what did his dates help him when Jack Simons of the lower third chivvied him down the passage with the buckle end of a strap? But you didn't do things like that with Jim Horscroft. What tales we used to whisper about his strength! How he put his fist through the oak-panel of the game-room door; how, when Long Merridew was carrying the ball, he caught up Merridew, ball and all, and ran swiftly past every opponent to the goal. It did not seem fit to us that such a one as he should trouble his head about spondees and dactyls, or care to know who signed the Magna Charta. When he said in open class that King Alfred was the man, we little boys all felt that very likely it was so, and that perhaps Jim knew more about it than the man who wrote the book.

Well, it was this business of the burglar that drew his attention to me; for he patted me on my head, and said that I was a spunky little devil, which blew me out with pride for a week on end. For two years we were close friends, for all the gap that the years had made between us, and though in passion or in want of thought he did many a thing that

15

galled me, yet I loved him like a brother, and wept as much as would have filled an ink bottle when at last he went off to Edinburgh to study his father's profession. Five years after that did I tide at Birtwhistle's, and when I left had become cock myself, for I was wiry and as tough as whalebone, though I never ran to weight and sinew like my great predecessor. It was in Jubilee Year that I left Birtwhistle's, and then for three years I stayed at home learning the ways of the cattle; but still the ships and the armies were wrestling, and still the great shadow of Bonaparte lay across the country. How could I guess that I too should have a hand in lifting that shadow for ever from our people?

2

Cousin Edie of Eyemouth

Some years before, when I was still but a lad, there had come over to us upon a five weeks' visit the only daughter of my father's brother. Willie Calder had settled at Eyemouth as a maker of fishing nets, and he had made more out of twine than ever we were like to do out of the whin-bushes and sand-links of West Inch. So his daughter, Edie Calder, came over with a braw red frock and a five shilling bonnet, and a kist full of things that brought my dear mother's eyes out like a partan's. It was wonderful to see her so free with money, and she but a slip of a girl, paying the carrier man all that he asked and a whole twopence over, to which he had no claim. She made no more of drinking ginger-beer than we did of water, and she would have her sugar in her tea and butter with her bread just as if she had been English.

I took no great stock of girls at that time, for it was hard for me to see what they had been made for. There were none of us at Birtwhistle's that thought very much of them;

17

but the smallest laddies seemed to have the most sense, for after they began to grow bigger they were not so sure about it. We little ones were all of one mind: that a creature that couldn't fight and was aye carrying tales, and couldn't so much as shy a stone without flapping its arm like a rag in the wind, was no use for anything. And then the airs that they would put on, as if they were mother and father rolled into one; for ever breaking into a game with 'Jimmy, your toe's come through your boot,' or 'Go home, you dirty boy, and clean yourself,' until the very sight of them was weariness.

So when this one came to the steading at West Inch I was not best pleased to see her. I was twelve at the time (it was in the holidays) and she eleven, a thin, tallish girl with black eyes and the queerest ways. She was for ever staring out in front of her with her lips parted, as if she saw something wonderful; but when I came behind her and looked the same way, I could see nothing but the sheep's trough or the midden, or father's breeches hanging on a clothes-line. And then if she saw a lump of heather or bracken, or any common stuff of that sort, she would mope over it, as if it had struck her sick, and cry, 'How sweet! how perfect!' just as though it had been a painted picture. She didn't like games, but I

18

used to make her play 'tig' and such like; but it was no fun, for I could always catch her in three jumps, and she could never catch me, though she would come with as much rustle and flutter as ten boys would make. When I used to tell her that she was good for nothing, and that her father was a fool to bring her up like that, she would begin to cry, and say that I was a rude boy, and that she would go home that very night, and never forgive me as long as she lived. But in five minutes she had forgot all about it. What was strange was that she liked me a deal better than I did her, and she would never leave me alone; but she was always watching me and running after me, and then saying, 'Oh, here you are!' as if it were a surprise.

But soon I found that there was good in her too. She used sometimes to give me pennies, so that once I had four in my pocket all at the same time; but the best part of her was the stories that she could tell. She was sore frightened of frogs, so I would bring one to her, and tell her that I would put it down her neck unless she told a story. That always helped her to begin; but when once she was started it was wonderful how she would carry on. And the things that had happened to her, they were enough to take your breath away. There was a Barbary rover that had been at

Eyemouth, and he was coming back in five years in a ship full of gold to make her his wife; and then there was a wandering knight who had been there also, and he had given her a ring which he said he would redeem when the time came. She showed me the ring, which was very like the ones upon my bed curtain; but she said that this one was virgin gold. I asked her what the knight would do if he met the Barbary rover, and she told me that he would sweep his head from his shoulders. What they could all see in her was more than I could think. And then she told me that she had been followed on her way to West Inch by a disguised prince. I asked her how she knew it was a prince, and she said by his disguise. Another day she said that her father was preparing a riddle, and that when it was ready it would be put in the papers, and anyone who guessed it would have half his fortune and his daughter. I said that I was good at riddles, and that she must send it to me when it was ready. She said it would be in the *Berwick Gazette*, and wanted to know what I would do with her when I won her. I said I would sell her by public roup for what she would fetch; but she would tell no more stories that evening, for she was very techy about some things.

Jim Horscroft was away when Cousin Edie

was with us, but he came back the very week she went; and I mind how surprised I was that he should ask any questions or take any interest in a mere lassie. He asked me if she were pretty; and when I said I hadn't noticed, he laughed and called me a mole, and said my eyes would be opened some day. But very soon he came to be interested in something else, and I never gave Edie another thought until one day she just took my life in her hands and twisted it as I could twist this quill.

That was in 1813, after I had left school, when I was already eighteen years of age, with a good forty hairs on my upper lip and every hope of more. I had changed since I left school, and was not so keen on games as I had been, but found myself instead lying about on the sunny side of the braes, with my own lips parted and my eyes staring just the same as Cousin Edie's used to do. It had satisfied me and filled my whole life that I could run faster and jump higher than my neighbour; but now all that seemed such a little thing, and I yearned, and yearned, and looked up at the big arching sky, and down at the flat blue sea, and felt that there was something wanting, but could never lay my tongue to what that something was. And I became quick of temper too, for my nerves seemed all of a fret, and when my mother would ask me what ailed me, or my father would speak of my turning my hand to work, I would break into such sharp bitter answers as I have often grieved over since. Ah! a man may have more than one wife, and more than one child, and more than one friend; but he can never have but the one mother, so let him cherish her while he may.

One day when I came in from the sheep, there was my father sitting with a letter in his hands, which was a very rare thing with us, except when the factor wrote for the rent. Then as I came nearer to him I saw that he was crying, and I stood staring, for I had always thought that it was not a thing that a man could do. I can see him now, for he had so deep a crease across his brown cheek that no tear could pass it, but must trickle away sideways and so down to his ear, hopping off on to the sheet of paper. My mother sat beside him and stroked his hands like she did the cat's back when she would soothe it.

'Aye, Jeannie,' said he, 'poor Willie's gone. It's from the lawyer, and it was sudden or they'd ha' sent word of it. Carbuncle, he says, and a flush o' blood to the head.'

'Ah! well, his trouble's over,' said my mother.

My father rubbed his ears with the tablecloth.

'He's left a' his savings to his lassie,' said he, 'and by gom if she's not changed from what she promised to be she'll soon gar them flee. You mind what she said of weak tea under this very roof, and it at seven shillings the pound!'

My mother shook her head, and looked up at the flitches of bacon that hung from the ceiling.

'He doesn't say how much, but she'll have enough and to spare, he says. And she's to come and bide with us, for that was his last wish.'

'To pay for her keep!' cried my mother sharply. I was sorry that she should have spoken of money at that moment, but then if she had not been sharp we would all have been on the roadside in a twelvemonth.

'Aye, she'll pay, and she's coming this very day. Jock lad, I'll want you to drive to Ayton and meet the evening coach. Your Cousin Edie will be in it, and you can fetch her over to West Inch.'

And so off I started at quarter past five with Souter Johnnie, the long-haired fifteen-year-old, and our cart with the new-painted tail-board that we only used on great days. The coach was in just as I came, and I, like a foolish country lad, taking no heed to the years that had passed, was looking about

23

among the folk in the Inn front for a slip of a girl with her petticoats just under her knees. And as I slouched past and craned my neck there came a touch to my elbow, and there was a lady dressed all in black standing by the steps, and I knew that it was my cousin Edie.

I knew it, I say, and yet had she not touched me I might have passed her a score of times and never known it. My word, if Jim Horscroft had asked me then if she were pretty or no, I should have known how to answer him! She was dark, much darker than is common among our border lasses, and yet with such a faint blush of pink breaking through her dainty colour, like the deeper flush at the heart of a sulphur rose. Her lips were red, and kindly, and firm; and even then, at the first glance, I saw that light of mischief and mockery that danced away at the back of her great dark eyes. She took me then and there as though I had been her heritage, put out her hand and plucked me. She was, as I have said, in black, dressed in what seemed to me to be a wondrous fashion, with a black veil pushed up from her brow.

'Ah! Jack,' said she, in a mincing English fashion, that she had learned at the boarding school. 'No, no, we are rather old for that' — this because I in my awkward fashion was pushing my foolish brown face forward to kiss her, as I had done when I saw her last. 'Just hurry up like a good fellow and give a shilling to the conductor, who has been exceedingly civil to me during the journey.'

I flushed up red to the ears, for I had only a silver fourpenny piece in my pocket. Never had my lack of pence weighed so heavily upon me as just at that moment. But she read me at a glance, and there in an instant was a little moleskin purse with a silver clasp thrust into my hand. I paid the man, and would have given it back, but she still would have me keep it.

'You shall be my factor, Jack,' said she, laughing. 'Is this our carriage? How funny it looks! And where am I to sit?'

'On the sacking,' said I.

'And how am I to get there?'

'Put your foot on the hub,' said I. 'I'll help you.'

I sprang up and took her two little gloved hands in my own. As she came over the side her breath blew in my face, sweet and warm, and all that vagueness and unrest seemed in a moment to have been shredded away from my soul. I felt as if that instant had taken me out from myself, and made me one of the race. It took but the time of the flicking of the horse's tail, and yet something had happened, a barrier had gone down somewhere, and I was leading a wider and a wiser life. I felt it all in a flush, but shy and backward as I was, I could do nothing but flatten out the sacking for her. Her eyes were after the coach which was rattling away to Berwick, and suddenly she shook her handkerchief in the air.

'He took off his hat,' said she. 'I think he must have been an officer. He was very distinguished looking. Perhaps you noticed him — a gentleman on the outside, very handsome, with a brown overcoat.'

I shook my head, with all my flush of joy changed to foolish resentment.

'Ah! well, I shall never see him again. Here are all the green braes and the brown winding road just the same as ever. And you, Jack, I don't see any great change in you either. I hope your manners are better than they used to be. You won't try to put any frogs down my back, will you?'

I crept all over when I thought of such a thing.

'We'll do all we can to make you happy at West Inch,' said I, playing with the whip.

'I'm sure it's very kind of you to take a poor lonely girl in,' said she.

'It's very kind of you to come, Cousin Edie,' I stammered. 'You'll find it very dull, I fear.'

'I suppose it is a little quiet, Jack, eh? Not many men about, as I remember it.'

'There is Major Elliott, up at Corriemuir. He comes down of an evening, a real brave old soldier who had a ball in his knee under Wellington.'

'Ah, when I speak of men. Jack, I don't mean old folk with balls in their knees. I meant people of our own age that we could make friends of. By the way, that crabbed old doctor had a son, had he not?'

'Oh yes, that's Jim Horscroft, my best friend.'

'Is he at home?'

'No. He'll be home soon. He's still at Edinburgh studying.'

'Ah! then we'll keep each other company until he comes, Jack. And I'm very tired and I wish I was at West Inch.'

I made old Souter Johnnie cover the ground as he has never done before or since, and in an hour she was seated at the supper table, where my mother had laid out not only butter, but a glass dish of gooseberry jam, which sparkled and looked fine in the candle-light. I could see that my parents were as overcome as I was at the difference in her, though not in the same way. My mother was so set back by the feather thing that she had round her neck that she called her Miss

Calder instead of Edie, until my cousin in her pretty flighty way would lift her forefinger to her whenever she did it. After supper, when she had gone to bed, they could talk of nothing but her looks and her breeding.

'By the way, though,' says my father, 'it does not look as if she were heart-broke about my brother's death.'

And then for the first time I remembered that she had never said a word about the matter since I had met her.

3

The Shadow on the Waters

It was not very long before Cousin Edie was queen of West Inch, and we all her devoted subjects from my father down. She had money and to spare, though none of us knew how much. When my mother said that four shillings the week would cover all that she would cost, she fixed on seven shillings and sixpence of her own free will. The south room, which was the sunniest and had the honeysuckle round the window, was for her; and it was a marvel to see the things that she brought from Berwick to put into it. Twice a week she would drive over, and the cart would not do for her, for she hired a gig from Angus Whitehead, whose farm lay over the hill. And it was seldom that she went without bringing something back for one or other of us. It was a wooden pipe for my father, or a Shetland plaid for my mother, or a book for me, or a brass collar for Rob the collie. There was never a woman more freehanded.

But the best thing that she gave us was just her own presence. To me it changed the whole country-side, and the sun was brighter and the braes greener and the air sweeter from the day she came. Our lives were common no longer now that we spent them with such a one as she, and the old dull grey house was another place in my eyes since she had set her foot across the door-mat. It was not her face, though that was winsome enough, nor her form, though I never saw the lass that could match her; but it was her spirit, her queer mocking ways, her fresh new fashion of talk, her proud whisk of the dress and toss of the head, which made one feel like the ground beneath her feet, and then the quick challenge in her eye, and the kindly word that brought one up to her level again.

But never quite to her level either. To me she was always something above and beyond. I might brace myself and blame myself, and do what I would, but still I could not feel that the same blood ran in our veins, and that she was but a country lassie, as I was a country lad. The more I loved her the more frightened I was at her, and she could see the fright long before she knew the love. I was uneasy to be away from her, and yet when I was with her I was in a shiver all the time for fear my stumbling talk might weary her or give her offence. Had I known more of the ways of women I might have taken less pains.

'You're a deal changed from what you used to be, Jack,' said she, looking at me sideways from under her dark lashes.

'You said not when first we met,' says I.

'Ah! I was speaking of your looks then, and of your ways now. You used to be so rough to me, and so masterful, and would have your own way, like the little man that you were. I can see you now with your touzled brown hair and your mischievous eyes. And now you are so gentle and quiet and soft-spoken.'

'One learns to behave,' says I.

'Ah, but, Jack, I liked you so much better as you were!'

Well, when she said that I fairly stared at her, for I had thought that she could never have quite forgiven me for the way I used to carry on. That anyone out of a daft house could have liked it, was clean beyond my understanding. I thought of how when she was reading by the door I would go up on the moor with a hazel switch and fix little clay balls at the end of it, and sling them at her until I made her cry. And then I thought of how I caught an eel in the Corriemuir burn and chivvied her about with it, until she ran screaming under my mother's apron half mad with fright, and my father gave me one on the ear-hole with the porridge stick which knocked me and my eel under the kitchen dresser. And these were the things that she missed! Well, she must miss them, for my hand would wither before I could do them now. But for the first time I began to understand the queerness that lies in a woman, and that a man must not reason about one, but just watch and try to learn.

We found our level after a time, when she saw that she had just to do what she liked and how she liked, and that I was as much at her beck and call as old Rob was at mine. You'll think I was a fool to have had my head so turned, and maybe I was; but then you must think how little I was used to women, and how much we were thrown together. Besides she was a woman in a million, and I can tell you that it was a strong head that would not be turned by her.

Why, there was Major Elliott, a man that had buried three wives, and had twelve pitched battles to his name, Edie could have turned him round her finger like a damp rag — she, only new from the boarding school. I met him hobbling from West Inch the first time after she came, with pink in his cheeks and a shine in his eye that took ten years from him. He was cocking up his grey moustaches at either end and curling them into his eyes, and strutting out with his sound leg as proud as a piper. What she had said to him the Lord knows, but it was like old wine in his veins.

'I've been up to see you, laddie,' said he, 'but I must home again now. My visit has not been wasted, however, as I had an opportunity of seeing *la belle cousine*. A most charming and engaging young lady, laddie.'

He had a formal stiff way of talking, and was fond of jerking in a bit of the French, for he had picked some up in the Peninsula. He would have gone on talking of Cousin Edie, but I saw the corner of a newspaper thrusting out of his pocket, and I knew that he had come over, as was his way, to give me some news, for we heard little enough at West Inch.

'What is fresh, Major?' I asked. He pulled the paper out with a flourish.

'The allies have won a great battle, my lad,' says he. 'I don't think Nap can stand up long against this. The Saxons have thrown him over, and he's been badly beat at Leipzig. Wellington is past the Pyrenees, and Graham's folk will be at Bayonne before long.'

I chucked up my hat.

'Then the war will come to an end at last,' I cried.

'Aye, and time too,' said he, shaking his head gravely. 'It's been a bloody business. But it is hardly worthwhile for me to say now what was in my mind about you.'

'What was that?'

'Well, laddie, you are doing no good here, and now that my knee is getting more limber I was hoping that I might get on active service again. I wondered whether maybe you might like to do a little soldiering under me.'

My heart jumped at the thought.

'Aye, would I!' I cried.

'But it'll be clear six months before I'll be fit to pass a board, and it's long odds that Boney will be under lock and key before that.'

'And there's my mother,' said I, 'I doubt she'd ever let me go.'

'Ah! well, she'll never be asked to now,' he answered, and hobbled on upon his way.

I sat down among the heather with my chin on my hand, turning the thing over in my mind, and watching him in his old brown clothes, with the end of a grey plaid flapping over his shoulder, as he picked his way up the swell of the hill. It was a poor life this, at West Inch, waiting to fill my father's shoes, with the same heath, and the same burn, and the same sheep, and the same grey house for ever before me. But over there, over the blue sea, ah! there was a life fit for a man. There was the Major, a man past his prime, wounded and spent, and yet planning to get to work again, whilst I, with all the strength of my youth, was wasting it upon these hillsides. A hot wave of shame flushed over me, and I sprang up all in a tingle to be off and playing a man's part in the world.

For two days I turned it over in my mind, and on the third there came something which first brought all my resolutions to a head, and then blew them all to nothing like a puff of smoke in the wind.

I had strolled out in the afternoon with Cousin Edie and Rob, until we found ourselves upon the brow of the slope which dips away down to the beach. It was late in the fall, and the links were all bronzed and faded; but the sun still shone warmly, and a south breeze came in little hot pants, rippling the broad blue sea with white curling lines. I pulled an armful of bracken to make a couch for Edie, and there she lay in her listless fashion, happy and contented; for of all folk that I have ever met, she had the most joy from warmth and light. I leaned on a tussock of grass, with Rob's head upon my knee, and there as we sat alone in peace in the wilderness, even there we saw suddenly thrown upon the waters in front of us the shadow of that great man over yonder, who had scrawled his name in red letters across the map of Europe. There was a ship coming up with the wind, a black sedate old merchant-man, bound for Leith as likely as not. Her yards were square and she was running with all sail set. On the other tack, coming from the north-east, were two great ugly lugger-like craft, with one high mast each, and a big square brown sail. A prettier sight one would not wish than to see the three craft dipping along upon so fair a day. But of a sudden there came a spurt of flame and a whirl of blue smoke from one lugger, then the same from the second, and a rap, rap, rap, from the ship. In a twinkling hell had elbowed out heaven, and there on the waters was hatred and savagery and the lust for blood.

We had sprung to our feet at the outburst, and Edie put her hand all in a tremble upon my arm.

'They are fighting, Jack!' she cried. 'What are they? Who are they?'

My heart was thudding with the guns, and it was all that I could do to answer her for the catch of my breath.

'It's two French privateers, Edie,' said I, 'Chasse-marries, they call them, and yon's one of our merchant ships, and they'll take her as sure as death; for the Major says they've always got heavy guns, and are as full of men as an egg is full of meat. Why doesn't the fool make back for Tweedmouth bar?'

But not an inch of canvas did she lower, but floundered on in her stolid fashion, while a little black ball ran up to her peak, and the rare old flag streamed suddenly out from the halliard. Then again came the rap, rap, rap, of her little guns, and the boom, boom of the big carronades in the bows of the lugger. An instant later the three ships met, and the merchantman staggered on like a stag with two wolves hanging to its haunches. The three became but a dark blur amid the smoke, with the top spars thrusting out in a bristle, and from the heart of that cloud came the quick red flashes of flame, and such a devils' racket of big guns and small, cheering and scream-ing, as was to din in my head for many a week. For a stricken hour the hell-cloud moved slowly across the face of the water, and still with our hearts in our mouths we watched the flap of the flag, straining to see if it were yet there. And then suddenly, the ship, as proud and black and high as ever, shot on upon her way; and as the smoke cleared we saw one of the luggers squattering like a broken winged duck upon the water, and the other working hard to get the crew from her before she sank.

For all that hour I had lived for nothing but the fight. My cap had been whisked away by the wind, but I had never given it a thought. Now with my heart full I turned upon my Cousin Edie, and the sight of her took me back six years. There was the vacant staring eye and the parted lips, just as I had seen them in her girlhood, and her little hands were clenched until the knuckles gleamed like ivory.

'Ah, that captain!' said she, talking to the heath and the whin-bushes. 'There is a man so strong, so resolute! What woman would not be proud of a man like that?'

'Aye, he did well!' I cried with enthusiasm.

She looked at me as if she had forgotten my existence.

'I would give a year of my life to meet such a man,' said she. 'But that is what living in the country means. One never sees anybody but just those who are fit for nothing better.'

I do not know that she meant to hurt me, though she was never very backward at that; but whatever her intention, her words seemed to strike straight upon a naked nerve.

'Very well, Cousin Edie,' I said, trying to speak calmly, 'that puts the cap on it. I'll take the bounty in Berwick to-night.'

'What, Jack! you be a soldier!'

'Yes, if you think that every man that bides in the country must be a coward.'

'Oh, you'd look so handsome in a red coat, Jack, and it improves you vastly when you are in a temper. I wish your eyes would always flash like that, for it looks so nice and manly. But I am sure that you are joking about the soldiering.'

'I'll let you see if I am joking.'

Then and there I set off running over the moor, until I burst into the kitchen where my mother and father were sitting on either side of the ingle.

'Mother,' I cried, 'I'm off for a soldier!'

Had I said I was off for a burglar they could not have looked worse over it, for in those days among the decent canny country folks it was mostly the black sheep that were herded by the sergeant. But, my word, those same black sheep did their country some rare service too. My mother put up her mittens to her eyes, and my father looked as black as a peat hole.

'Hoots, Jock, you're daft,' says he.

'Daft or no, I'm going.'

'Then you'll have no blessing from me.'

'Then I'll go without.'

At this my mother gives a screech and throws her arms about my neck. I saw her hand, all hard and worn and knuckly with the work she had done for my up-bringing, and it pleaded with me as words could not have done. My heart was soft for her, but my will was as hard as a flint-edge. I put her back in her chair with a kiss, and then ran to my room to pack my bundle. It was already growing dark, and I had a long walk before me, so I thrust a few things together and hastened out. As I came through the side door someone touched my shoulder, and there was Edie in the gloaming.

'Silly boy,' said she, 'you are not really going.'

'Am I not? You'll see.'

'But your father does not wish it, nor your mother.'

'I know that.'

'Then why go?'

'You ought to know.'

'Why, then?'

'Because you make me!'

'I don't want you to go, Jack.'

'You said it. You said that the folk in the country were fit for nothing better. You always speak like that. You think no more of me than of those doos in the cot. You think I am nobody at all. I'll show you different.'

All my troubles came out in hot little spurts of speech. She coloured up as I spoke, and looked at me in her queer half-mocking, half-petting fashion.

'Oh, I think so little of you as that?' said she. 'And that is the reason why you are going away? Well then, Jack, will you stay if I am — if I am kind to you?'

We were face to face and close together, and in an instant the thing was done. My arms were round her, and I was kissing her,

40

and kissing her, and kissing her, on her mouth, her cheeks, her eyes, and pressing her to my heart, and whispering to her that she was all, all, to me, and that I could not be without her. She said nothing, but it was long before she turned her face aside, and when she pushed me back it was not very hard.

'Why, you are quite your rude, old, impudent self!' said she, patting her hair with her two hands. 'You have tossed me, Jack; I had no idea that you would be so forward!'

But all my fear of her was gone, and a love tenfold hotter than ever was boiling in my veins. I took her up again, and kissed her as if it were my right.

'You are my very own now!' I cried. 'I shall not go to Berwick, but I'll stay and marry you.'

But she laughed when I spoke of marriage.

'Silly boy! Silly boy!' said she, with her forefinger up; and then when I tried to lay hands on her again, she gave a little dainty curtsy, and was off into the house.

4

The Choosing of Jim

And then there came those ten weeks which were like a dream, and are so now to look back upon. I would weary you were I to tell you what passed between us; but oh, how earnest and fateful and all-important it was at the time! Her waywardness; her ever-varying moods, now bright, now dark, like a meadow under drifting clouds; her causeless angers; her sudden repentances, each in turn filling me with joy or sorrow: these were my life, and all the rest was but emptiness. But ever deep down behind all my other feelings was a vague disquiet, a fear that I was like the man who set forth to lay hands upon the rainbow, and that the real Edie Calder, however near she might seem, was in truth for ever beyond my reach.

For she was so hard to understand, or, at least, she was so for a dull-witted country lad like me. For if I would talk to her of my real prospects, and how by taking in the whole of Corriemuir we might earn a hundred good pounds over the extra rent, and maybe be able to build out the parlour at West Inch, so as to make it fine for her when we married, she would pout her lips and droop her eyes, as though she scarce had patience to listen to me. But if I would let her build up dreams about what I might become, how I might find a paper which proved me to be the true heir of the laird, or how, without joining the army, which she would by no means hear of, I showed myself to be a great warrior until my name was in all folks' mouths, then she would be as blithe as the May. I would keep up the play as well as I could, but soon some luckless word would show that I was only plain Jock Calder of West Inch, and out would come her lip again in scorn of me. So we moved on, she in the air and I on the ground; and if the rift had not come in one way, it must in another.

It was after Christmas, but the winter had been mild, with just frost enough to make it safe walking over the peat bogs. One fresh morning Edie had been out early, and she came back to breakfast with a fleck of colour on her cheeks.

'Has your friend the doctor's son come home, Jack?' says she.

'I heard that it was expected.'

'Ah! then it must have been him that I met on the muir.'

'What! you met Jim Horscroft?'

43

'I am sure it must be he. A splendid-looking man — a hero, with curly black hair, a short, straight nose, and grey eyes. He had shoulders like a statue, and as to height, why, I suppose that your head, Jack, would come up to his scarf-pin.'

'Up to his ear, Edie!' said I indignantly. 'That is, if it was Jim. But tell me. Had he a brown wooden pipe stuck in the corner of his mouth?'

'Yes, he was smoking. He was dressed in grey, and he has a grand deep strong voice.'

'Ho, ho! you spoke to him!' said I.

She coloured a little, as if she had said more than she meant.

'I was going where the ground was a little soft, and he warned me of it,' she said.

'Ah! it must have been dear old Jim,' said I. 'He should have been a doctor years back, if his brains had been as strong as his arm. Why, heart alive, here is the very man himself!'

I had seen him through the kitchen window, and now I rushed out with my half-eaten bannock in my hand to greet him. He ran forward too, with his great hand out and his eyes shining.

'Ah! Jock,' he cried, 'it's good to see you again. There are no friends like the old ones.'

Then suddenly he stuck in his speech, and stared with his mouth open over my shoulder.

I turned, and there was Edie, with such a merry, roguish smile, standing in the door. How proud I felt of her, and of myself too, as I looked at her!

'This is my cousin, Miss Edie Calder, Jim,' said I.

'Do you often take walks before breakfast, Mr. Horscroft?' she asked, still with that roguish smile.

'Yes,' said he, staring at her with all his eyes.

'So do I, and generally over yonder,' said she. 'But you are not very hospitable to your friend, Jack. If you do not do the honours, I shall have to take your place for the credit of West Inch.'

Well, in another minute we were in with the old folk, and Jim had his plate of porridge ladled out for him; but hardly a word would he speak, but sat with his spoon in his hand staring at Cousin Edie. She shot little twinkling glances across at him all the time, and it seemed to me that she was amused at his backwardness, and that she tried by what she said to give him heart.

'Jack was telling me that you were studying to be a doctor,' said she. 'But oh, how hard it must be, and how long it must take before one can gather so much learning as that!'

'It takes me long enough,' Jim answered

ruefully; 'but I'll beat it yet.'

'Ah! but you are brave. You are resolute. You fix your eyes on a point and you move on towards it, and nothing can stop you.'

'Indeed, I've little to boast of,' said he. 'Many a one who began with me has put up his plate years ago, and here am I but a student still.'

'That is your modesty, Mr. Horscroft. They say that the bravest are always humble. But then, when you have gained your end, what a glorious career — to carry healing in your hands, to raise up the suffering, to have for one's sole end the good of humanity!'

Honest Jim wriggled in his chair at this.

'I'm afraid I have no such very high motives, Miss Calder,' said he. 'It's to earn a living, and to take over my father's business, that I do it. If I carry healing in one hand, I have the other out for a crown-piece.'

'How candid and truthful you are!' she cried; and so they went on, she decking him with every virtue, and twisting his words to make him play the part, in the way that I knew so well. Before he was done I could see that his head was buzzing with her beauty and her kindly words. I thrilled with pride to think that he should think so well of my kin.

'Isn't she fine, Jim?' I could not help saying when we stood outside the door, he lighting his pipe before he set off home.

'Fine!' he cried; 'I never saw her match!'

'We're going to be married,' said I.

The pipe fell out of his mouth, and he stood staring at me. Then he picked it up and walked off without a word. I thought that he would likely come back, but he never did; and I saw him far off up the brae, with his chin on his chest.

But I was not to forget him, for Cousin Edie had a hundred questions to ask me about his boyhood, about his strength, about the women that he was likely to know; there was no satisfying her. And then again, later in the day, I heard of him, but in a less pleasant fashion.

It was my father who came home in the evening with his mouth full of poor Jim. He had been deadly drunk since midday, had been down to Westhouse Links to fight the gipsy champion, and it was not certain that the man would live through the night. My father had met Jim on the highroad, dour as a thunder-cloud, and with an insult in his eye for every man that passed him. 'Guid sakes!' said the old man. 'He'll make a fine practice for himsel', if breaking banes will do it.'

Cousin Edie laughed at all this, and I laughed because she did; but I was not so sure that it was funny.

On the third day afterwards, I was going up Corriemuir by the sheep-track, when who should I see striding down but Jim himself. But he was a different man from the big, kindly fellow who had supped his porridge with us the other morning. He had no collar nor tie, his vest was open, his hair matted, and his face mottled, like a man who has drunk heavily overnight. He carried an ash stick, and he slashed at the whin-bushes on either side of the path.

'Why, Jim!' said I.

But he looked at me in the way that I had often seen at school when the devil was strong in him, and when he knew that he was in the wrong, and yet set his will to brazen it out. Not a word did he say, but he brushed past me on the narrow path and swaggered on, still brandishing his ash-plant and cutting at the bushes.

Ah well, I was not angry with him. I was sorry, very sorry, and that was all. Of course I was not so blind but that I could see how the matter stood. He was in love with Edie, and he could not bear to think that I should have her. Poor devil, how could he help it? Maybe I should have been the same. There was a time when I should have wondered that a girl could have turned a strong man's head like that, but I knew more about it now.

For a fortnight I saw nothing of Jim Horscroft, and then came the Thursday which was to change the whole current of my life.

I had woke early that day, and with a little thrill of joy which is a rare thing to feel when a man first opens his eyes. Edie had been kinder than usual the night before, and I had fallen asleep with the thought that maybe at last I had caught the rainbow, and that without any imaginings or make-believes she was learning to love plain, rough Jock Calder of West Inch. It was this thought, still at my heart, which had given me that little morning chirrup of joy. And then I remembered that if I hastened I might be in time for her, for it was her custom to go out with the sunrise.

But I was too late. When I came to her door it was half-open and the room empty. Well, thought I, at least I may meet her and have the homeward walk with her. From the top of Corriemuir hill you may see all the country round; so, catching up my stick, I swung off in that direction. It was bright, but cold, and the surf, I remember, was booming loudly, though there had been no wind in our parts for days. I zigzagged up the steep pathway, breathing in the thin, keen morning air, and humming a lilt as I went, until I came out, a little short of breath, among the whins

49

upon the top. Looking down the long slope of the farther side, I saw Cousin Edie, as I had expected; and I saw Jim Horscroft walking by her side.

They were not far away, but too taken up with each other to see me. She was walking slowly, with the little petulant cock of her dainty head which I knew so well, casting her eyes away from him, and shooting out a word from time to time. He paced along beside her, looking down at her and bending his head in the eagerness of his talk. Then as he said something, she placed her hand with a caress upon his arm, and he, carried off his feet, plucked her up and kissed her again and again. At the sight I could neither cry out nor move, but stood, with a heart of lead and the face of a dead man, staring down at them. I saw her hand passed over his shoulder, and that his kisses were as welcome to her as ever mine had been.

Then he set her down again, and I found that this had been their parting; for, indeed, in another hundred paces they would have come in view of the upper windows of the house. She walked slowly away, with a wave back once or twice, and he stood looking after her. I waited until she was someway off, and then down I came, but so taken up was he, that I was within a hand's-touch of him before he whisked round upon me. He tried to smile as his eye met mine.

'Ah, Jock,' says he, 'early afoot!'

'I saw you!' I gasped; and my throat had turned so dry that I spoke like a man with a quinsy.

'Did you so?' said he, and gave a little whistle. 'Well, on my life, Jock, I'm not sorry. I was thinking of coming up to West Inch this very day, and having it out with you. Maybe it's better as it is.'

'You've been a fine friend!' said I.

'Well now, be reasonable, Jock,' said he, sticking his hands into his pockets and rocking to and fro as he stood. 'Let me show you how it stands. Look me in the eye, and you'll see that I don't lie. It's this way. I had met Edie — Miss Calder that is — before I came that morning, and there were things which made me look upon her as free; and, thinking that, I let my mind dwell on her. Then you said she wasn't free, but was promised to you, and that was the worst knock I've had for a time. It clean put me off, and I made a fool of myself for some days, and it's a mercy I'm not in Berwick gaol. Then by chance I met her again — on my soul, Jock, it was chance for me — and when I spoke of you she laughed at the thought. It was cousin and cousin, she said; but as for

51

her not being free, or you being more to her than a friend, it was fool's talk. So you see, Jock, I was not so much to blame, after all: the more so as she promised that she would let you see by her conduct that you were mistaken in thinking that you had any claim upon her. You must have noticed that she has hardly had a word for you for these last two weeks.'

I laughed bitterly.

'It was only last night,' said I, 'that she told me that I was the only man in all this earth that she could ever bring herself to love.'

Jim Horscroft put out a shaking hand and laid it on my shoulder, while he pushed his face forward to look into my eyes.

'Jock Calder,' said he, 'I never knew you tell a lie. You are not trying to score trick against trick, are you? Honest now, between man and man.'

'It's God's truth,' said I.

He stood looking at me, and his face had set like that of a man who is having a hard fight with himself. It was a long two minutes before he spoke.

'See here, Jock!' said he. 'This woman is fooling us both. D'you hear, man? she's fooling us both! She loves you at West Inch, and she loves me on the braeside; and in her devil's heart she cares a whin-blossom for neither of us. Let's join hands, man, and send the hellfire hussy to the right-about!'

But this was too much. I could not curse her in my own heart, and still less could I stand by and hear another man do it; not though it was my oldest friend.

'Don't you call names!' I cried.

'Ach! you sicken me with your soft talk! I'll call her what she should be called!'

'Will you, though?' said I, lugging off my coat. 'Look you here, Jim Horscroft, if you say another word against her, I'll lick it down your throat, if you were as big as Berwick Castle! Try me and see!'

He peeled off his coat down to the elbows, and then he slowly put it on again.

'Don't be such a fool, Jock!' said he. 'Four stone and five inches is more than mortal man can give. Two old friends mustn't fall out over such a — well, there, I won't say it. Well, by the Lord, if she hasn't nerve for ten!'

I looked round, and there she was, not twenty yards from us, looking as cool and easy and placid as we were hot and fevered.

'I was nearly home,' said she, 'when I saw you two boys very busy talking, so I came all the way back to know what it was about.'

Horscroft took a run forward and caught her by the wrist. She gave a little squeal at the sight of his face, but he pulled her towards

53

where I was standing.

'Now, Jock, we've had tomfoolery enough,' said he. 'Here she is. Shall we take her word as to which she likes? She can't trick us now that we're both together.'

'I am willing,' said I.

'And so am I. If she goes for you, I swear I'll never so much as turn an eye on her again. Will you do as much for me?'

'Yes, I will.'

'Well then, look here, you! We're both honest men, and friends, and we tell each other no lies; and so we know your double ways. I know what you said last night. Jock knows what you said to-day. D'you see? Now then, fair and square! Here we are before you; once and have done. Which is it to be, Jock or me?'

You would have thought that the woman would have been overwhelmed with shame, but instead of that her eyes were shining with delight; and I dare wager that it was the proudest moment of her life. As she looked from one to the other of us, with the cold morning sun glittering on her face, I had never seen her look so lovely. Jim felt it also, I am sure; for he dropped her wrist, and the harsh lines were softened upon his face.

'Come, Edie! which is it to be?' he asked.

'Naughty boys, to fall out like this!' she

cried. 'Cousin Jack, you know how fond I am of you.'

'Oh, then go to him!' said Horscroft.

'But I love nobody but Jim. There is nobody that I love like Jim.'

She snuggled up to him, and laid her cheek against his breast.

'You see, Jock!' said he, looking over her shoulder.

I did see; and away I went for West Inch, another man from the time that I left it.

5

The Man From the Sea

Well, I was never one to sit groaning over a cracked pot. If it could not be mended, then it is the part of a man to say no more of it. For weeks I had an aching heart; indeed, it is a little sore now, after all these years and a happy marriage, when I think of it. But I kept a brave face on me; and, above all, I did as I had promised that day on the hillside. I was as a brother to her, and no more: though there were times when I had to put a hard curb upon myself; for even now she would come to me with her coaxing ways, and with tales about how rough Jim was, and how happy she had been when I was kind to her; for it was in her blood to speak like that, and she could not help it.

But for the most part Jim and she were happy enough. It was all over the countryside that they were to be married when he had passed his degree, and he would come up to West Inch four nights a week to sit with us. My folk were pleased about it, and I tried to be pleased too.

Maybe at first there was a little coolness between him and me: there was not quite the old schoolboy trust between us. But then, when the first smart was passed, it seemed to me that he had acted openly, and that I had no just cause for complaint against him. So we were friendly, in a way; and as for her, he had forgotten all his anger, and would have kissed the print of her shoe in the mud. We used to take long rambles together, he and I; and it is about one of these that I now want to tell you.

We had passed over Bramston Heath and round the clump of firs which screens the house of Major Elliott from the sea wind. It was spring now, and the year was a forward one, so that the trees were well leaved by the end of April. It was as warm as a summer day, and we were the more surprised when we saw a huge fire roaring upon the grass-plot before the Major's door. There was half a fir-tree in it, and the flames were spouting up as high as the bedroom windows. Jim and I stood staring, but we stared the more when out came the Major, with a great quart pot in his hand, and at his heels his old sister who kept house for him, and two of the maids, and all four began capering about round the fire. He was a douce, quiet man, as all the country knew, and here he was like old Nick

57

at the carlin's dance, hobbling around and waving his drink above his head. We both set off running, and he waved the more when he saw us coming.

'Peace!' he roared. 'Huzza, boys! Peace!'

And at that we both fell to dancing and shouting too; for it had been such a weary war as far back as we could remember, and the shadow had lain so long over us, that it was wondrous to feel that it was lifted. Indeed it was too much to believe, but the Major laughed our doubts to scorn.

'Aye, aye, it is true,' he cried, stopping with his hand to his side. 'The Allies have got Paris, Boney has thrown up the sponge, and his people are all swearing allegiance to Louis XVIII.'

'And the Emperor?' I asked. 'Will they spare him?'

'There's talk of sending him to Elba, where he'll be out of mischief's way. But his officers, there are some of them who will not get off so lightly. Deeds have been done during these last twenty years that have not been forgotten. There are a few old scores to be settled. But it's Peace! Peace!'

And away he went once more with his great tankard hopping round his bonfire.

Well, we stayed some time with the Major, and then away we went down to the beach,

Jim and I, talking about this great news, and all that would come of it. He knew a little, and I knew less, but we pieced it all together and talked about how the prices would come down, how our brave fellows would return home, how the ships could go where they would in peace, and how we could pull all the coast beacons down, for there was no enemy now to fear. So we chatted as we walked along the clean, hard sand, and looked out at the old North Sea. How little did Jim know at that moment, as he strode along by my side so full of health and of spirits, that he had reached the extreme summit of his life, and that from that hour all would, in truth, be upon the downward slope!

There was a little haze out to sea; for it had been very misty in the early morning, though the sun had thinned it. As we looked seawards we suddenly saw the sail of a small boat break out through the fog, and come bobbing along towards the land. A single man was seated in the sheets, and she yawed about as she ran, as though he were of two minds whether to beach her or no. At last, determined it may be by our presence, he made straight for us, and her keel grated upon the shingle at our very feet. He dropped his sail, sprang out, and pulled her bows up on the beach.

'Great Britain, I believe?' said he, turning

briskly round and facing us.

He was a man somewhat above middle height, but exceedingly thin. His eyes were piercing and set close together, a long sharp nose jutted out from between them, and beneath them was a bristle of brown moustache as wiry and stiff as a cat's whiskers. He was well dressed in a suit of brown with brass buttons, and he wore high boots which were all roughened and dulled by the sea water. His face and hands were so dark that he might have been a Spaniard, but as he raised his hat to us we saw that the upper part of his brow was quite white and that it was from without that he had his swarthiness. He looked from one to the other of us, and his grey eyes had something in them which I had never seen before. You could read the question; but there seemed to be a menace at the back of it, as if the answer were a right and not a favour.

'Great Britain?' he asked again, with a quick tap of his foot on the shingle.

'Yes,' said I, while Jim burst out laughing.

'England? Scotland?'

'Scotland. But it's England past yonder trees.'

'*Bon!* I know where I am now. I've been in a fog without a compass for nearly three days, and I didn't thought I was ever to see land again.'

He spoke English glibly enough, but with some strange turn of speech from time to time.

'Where did you come from then?' asked Jim.

'I was in a ship that was wrecked,' said he shortly. 'What is the town down yonder?'

'It is Berwick.'

'Ah! well, I must get stronger before I can go further.'

He turned towards the boat, and as he did so he gave a lurch, and would have fallen had he not caught the prow. On this he seated himself and looked round with a face that was flushed, and two eyes that blazed like a wild beast's.

'*Voltigeurs de la Garde*,' he roared in a voice like a trumpet call, and then again '*Voltigeurs de la Garde!*'

He waved his hat above his head, and suddenly pitching forwards upon his face on the sand, he lay all huddled into a little brown heap.

Jim Horscroft and I stood and stared at each other. The coming of the man had been so strange, and his questions, and now this sudden turn. We took him by a shoulder each and turned him upon his back. There he lay with his jutting nose and his cat's whiskers, but his lips were bloodless, and his breath would scarce shake a feather.

'He's dying, Jim!' I cried.

'Aye, for want of food and water. There's not a drop or crumb in the boat. Maybe there's something in the bag.'

He sprang and brought out a black leather bag, which with a large blue coat was the only thing in the boat. It was locked, but Jim had it open in an instant. It was half full of gold pieces.

Neither of us had ever seen so much before — no, nor a tenth part of it. There must have been hundreds of them, all bright new British sovereigns. Indeed, so taken up were we that we had forgotten all about their owner until a groan took our thoughts back to him. His lips were bluer than ever, and his jaw had dropped. I can see his open mouth now, with its row of white wolfish teeth.

'My God, he's off!' cried Jim. 'Here, run to the burn, Jock, for a hatful of water. Quick, man, or he's gone! I'll loosen his things the while.' Away I tore, and was back in a minute with as much water as would stay in my Glengarry. Jim had pulled open the man's coat and shirt, and we doused the water over him, and forced some between his lips. It had a good effect; for after a gasp or two he sat up and rubbed his eyes slowly, like a man who is waking from a deep sleep. But neither Jim nor

I were looking at his face now, for our eyes were fixed upon his uncovered chest.

There were two deep red puckers in it, one just below the collar bone, and the other about half-way down on the right side. The skin of his body was extremely white up to the brown line of his neck, and the angry crinkled spots looked the more vivid against it. From above I could see that there was a corresponding pucker in the back at one place, but not at the other. Inexperienced as I was, I could tell what that meant. Two bullets had pierced his chest; one had passed through it, and the other had remained inside.

But suddenly he staggered up to his feet, and pulled his shirt to, with a quick suspicious glance at us.

'What have I been doing?' he asked. 'I've been off my head. Take no notice of anything I may have said. Have I been shouting?'

'You shouted just before you fell.'

'What did I shout?'

I told him, though it bore little meaning to my mind. He looked sharply at us, and then he shrugged his shoulders.

'It's the words of a song,' said he. 'Well, the question is, What am I to do now? I didn't thought I was so weak. Where did you get the water?'

I pointed towards the burn, and he staggered off to the bank. There he lay down upon his face, and he drank until I thought he would never have done. His long skinny neck was outstretched like a horse's, and he made a loud supping noise with his lips. At last he got up with a long sigh, and wiped his moustache with his sleeve.

'That's better,' said he. 'Have you any food?'

I had crammed two bits of oat-cake into my pocket when I left home, and these he crushed into his mouth and swallowed. Then he squared his shoulders, puffed out his chest, and patted his ribs with the flat of his hands.

'I am sure that I owe you exceedingly well,' said he. 'You have been very kind to a stranger. But I see that you have had occasion to open my bag.'

'We hoped that we might find wine or brandy there when you fainted.'

'Ah! I have nothing there but just a little — how do you say it? — my savings. They are not much, but I must live quietly upon them until I find something to do. Now one could live quietly here, I should say. I could not have come upon a more peaceful place, without perhaps so much as a *gendarme* nearer than that town.'

'You haven't told us yet who you are, where you come from, nor what you have been,' said Jim bluntly.

The stranger looked him up and down with a critical eye:

'My word, but you would make a grenadier for a flank company,' said he. 'As to what you ask, I might take offence at it from other lips; but you have a right to know, since you have received me with so great courtesy. My name is Bonaventure de Lapp. I am a soldier and a wanderer by trade, and I have come from Dunkirk, as you may see printed upon the boat.'

'I thought that you had been shipwrecked!' said I.

But he looked at me with the straight gaze of an honest man.

'That is right,' said he, 'but the ship went from Dunkirk, and this is one of her boats. The crew got away in the long boat, and she went down so quickly that I had no time to put anything into her. That was on Monday.'

'And to-day's Thursday. You have been three days without bite or sup.'

'It is too long,' said he. 'Twice before I have been for two days, but never quite so long as this. Well, I shall leave my boat here, and see whether I can get lodgings in any of these little grey houses upon the hillsides. Why is that great fire burning over yonder?'

'It is one of our neighbours who has served against the French. He is rejoicing because peace has been declared.'

'Oh, you have a neighbour who has served then! I am glad; for I, too, have seen a little soldiering here and there.'

He did not look glad, but he drew his brows down over his keen eyes.

'You are French, are you not?' I asked, as we all walked up the hill together, he with his black bag in his hand and his long blue cloak slung over his shoulder.

'Well, I am of Alsace,' said he; 'and, you know, they are more German than French. For myself, I have been in so many lands that I feel at home in all. I have been a great traveller; and where do you think that I might find a lodging?'

I can scarcely tell now, on looking back with the great gap of five-and-thirty years between, what impression this singular man had made upon me. I distrusted him, I think, and yet I was fascinated by him also; for there was something in his bearing, in his look, and his whole fashion of speech which was entirely unlike anything that I had ever seen. Jim Horscroft was a fine man, and Major Elliott was a brave one, but they both lacked something that this wanderer had. It was the

66

quick alert look, the flash of the eye, the nameless distinction which is so hard to fix. And then we had saved him when he lay gasping upon the shingle, and one's heart always softens towards what one has once helped.

'If you will come with me,' said I, 'I have little doubt that I can find you a bed for a night or two, and by that time you will be better able to make your own arrangements.'

He pulled off his hat, and bowed with all the grace imaginable. But Jim Horscroft pulled me by the sleeve, and led me aside.

'You're mad, Jock,' he whispered. 'The fellow's a common adventurer. What do you want to get mixed up with him for?'

But I was as obstinate a man as ever laced his boots, and if you jerked me back it was the finest way of sending me to the front.

'He's a stranger, and it's our part to look after him,' said I.

'You'll be sorry for it,' said he.

'Maybe so.'

'If you don't think of yourself, you might think of your cousin.'

'Edie can take very good care of herself.'

'Well, then, the devil take you, and you may do what you like!' he cried, in one of his sudden flushes of anger. Without a word of farewell to either of us, he turned off upon the track that led up towards his father's house. Bonaventure de Lapp smiled at me as we walked on together.

'I didn't thought he liked me very much,' said he. 'I can see very well that he has made a quarrel with you because you are taking me to your home. What does he think of me then? Does he think perhaps that I have stole the gold in my bag, or what is it that he fears?'

'Tut, I neither know nor care,' said I. 'No stranger shall pass our door without a crust and a bed.'

With my head cocked and feeling as if I was doing something very fine, instead of being the most egregious fool south of Edinburgh, I marched on down the path with my new acquaintance at my elbow.

6

A Wandering Eagle

My father seemed to be much of Jim Horscroft's opinion; for he was not over warm to this new guest and looked him up and down with a very questioning eye. He set a dish of vinegared herrings before him, however, and I noticed that he looked more askance than ever when my companion ate nine of them, for two were always our portion. When at last he had finished Bonaventure de Lapp's lids were drooping over his eyes, for I doubt that he had been sleepless as well as foodless for these three days. It was but a poor room to which I had led him, but he threw himself down upon the couch, wrapped his big blue cloak around him, and was asleep in an instant. He was a very high and strong snorer, and, as my room was next to his, I had reason to remember that we had a stranger within our gates.

When I came down in the morning, I found that he had been beforehand with me; for he was seated opposite my father at the window-table in the kitchen, their heads almost touching, and a little roll of gold pieces between them. As I came in my father looked up at me, and I saw a light of greed in his eyes such as I had never seen before. He caught up the money with an eager clutch and swept it into his pocket.

'Very good, mister,' said he; 'the room's yours, and you pay always on the third of the month.'

'Ah! and here is my first friend,' cried de Lapp, holding out his hand to me with a smile which was kindly enough, and yet had that touch of patronage which a man uses when he smiles to his dog. 'I am myself again now, thanks to my excellent supper and good night's rest. Ah! it is hunger that takes the courage from a man. That most, and cold next.'

'Aye, that's right,' said my father; 'I've been out on the moors in a snow-drift for six-and-thirty hours, and ken what it's like.'

'I once saw three thousand men starve to death,' remarked de Lapp, putting out his hands to the fire. 'Day by day they got thinner and more like apes, and they did come down to the edge of the pontoons where we did keep them, and they howled with rage and pain. The first few days their howls went over the whole city, but after a week our sentries on the bank could not hear them, so weak they had fallen.'

'And they died!' I exclaimed.

'They held out a very long time. Austrian Grenadiers they were, of the corps of Starowitz, fine stout men as big as your friend of yesterday; but when the town fell there were but four hundred alive, and a man could lift them three at a time as if they were little monkeys. It was a pity. Ah! my friend, you will do me the honours with madame and with mademoiselle.'

It was my mother and Edie who had come into the kitchen. He had not seen them the night before, but now it was all I could do to keep my face as I watched him; for instead of our homely Scottish nod, he bent up his back like a louping trout, and slid his foot, and clapped his hand over his heart in the queerest way. My mother stared, for she thought he was making fun of her; but Cousin Edie fell into it in an instant, as though it had been a game, and away she went in a great curtsy until I thought she would have had to give it up, and sit down right there in the middle of the kitchen floor. But no, she up again as light as a piece of fluff, and we all drew up our stools and started on the scones and milk and porridge.

He had a wonderful way with women, that man. Now if I were to do it, or Jim Horscroft, it would look as if we were playing the fool,

71

and the girls would have laughed at us; but with him it seemed to go with his style of face and fashion of speech, so that one came at last to look for it: for when he spoke to my mother or Cousin Edie — and he was never backward in speaking — it would always be with a bow and a look as if it would hardly be worth their while to listen to what he had to say, and when they answered he would put on a face as though every word they said was to be treasured up and remembered for ever. And yet, even while he humbled himself to a woman, there was always a proud sort of look at the back of his eye as if he meant to say that it was only to them that he was so meek, and that he could be stiff enough upon occasion. As to my mother, it was wonderful the way she softened to him, and in half-an-hour she had told him all about her uncle, who was a surgeon in Carlisle, and the highest of any upon her side of the house. She spoke to him about my brother Rob's death, which I had never heard her mention to a soul before, and he looked as if the tears were in his eyes over it — he, who had just told us how he had seen three thousand men starved to death! As to Edie, she did not say much, but she kept shooting little glances at our visitor, and once or twice he looked very hard at her.

When he had gone to his room after breakfast, my father pulled out eight golden pounds and laid them on the table. 'What think ye of that, Martha?' said he.

'You've sold the twa black tups after all.'

'No, but it's a month's pay for board and lodging from Jock's friend, and as much to come every four weeks.'

But my mother shook her head when she heard it.

'Two pounds a week is over much,' said she; 'and it is not when the poor gentleman is in distress that we should put such a price on his bit food.'

'Tut!' cried my father, 'he can very well afford it, and he with a bag full of gold. Besides, it's his own proposing.'

'No blessing will come from that money,' said she.

'Why, woman, he's turned your head wi' his foreign ways of speech!' cried my father.

'Aye, and it would be a good thing if Scottish men had a little more of that kindly way,' she said, and that was the first time in all my life that I had heard her answer him back.

He came down soon and asked me whether I would come out with him. When we were in the sunshine he held out a little cross made of red stones, one of the bonniest things that ever I had set eyes upon.

'These are rubies,' said he, 'and I got it at Tudela, in Spain. There were two of them, but I gave the other to a Lithuanian girl. I pray that you will take this as a memory of your exceedingly kindness to me yesterday. It will fashion into a pin for your cravat.'

I could but thank him for the present, which was of more value than anything I had ever owned in my life.

'I am off to the upper muir to count the lambs,' said I; 'maybe you would care to come up with me and see something of the country?'

He hesitated for a moment, and then he shook his head.

'I have some letters,' he said, 'which I ought to write as soon as possible. I think that I will stay at quiet this morning and get them written.'

All forenoon I was wandering over the links, and you may imagine that my mind was turning all the time upon this strange man whom chance had drifted to our doors. Where did he gain that style of his, that manner of command, that haughty menacing glint of the eye? And his experiences to which he referred so lightly, how wonderful the life must have been which had put him in the way of them! He had been kind to us, and gracious of speech, but still I could not quite shake myself clear of the distrust with which I had regarded him. Perhaps, after all, Jim Horscroft had been right and I had been wrong about taking him to West Inch.

When I got back he looked as though he had been born and bred in the steading. He sat in the big wooden-armed ingle-chair, with the black cat on his knee. His arms were out, and he held a skein of worsted from hand to hand which my mother was busily rolling into a ball. Cousin Edie was sitting near, and I could see by her eyes that she had been crying.

'Hullo, Edie!' said I, 'what's the trouble?'

'Ah! mademoiselle, like all good and true women, has a soft heart,' said he. 'I didn't thought it would have moved her, or I should have been silent. I have been talking of the suffering of some troops of which I knew something when they were crossing the Guadarama mountains in the winter of 1808. Ah! yes, it was very bad, for they were fine men and fine horses. It is strange to see men blown by the wind over the precipices, but the ground was so slippery and there was nothing to which they could hold. So companies all linked arms, and they did better in that fashion; but one artilleryman's hand came off as I held it, for he had had the frost-bite for three days.'

I stood staring with my mouth open.

'And the old Grenadiers, too, who were not so active as they used to be, they could not keep up; and yet if they lingered the peasants would catch them and crucify them to the barn doors with their feet up and a fire under their heads, which was a pity for these fine old soldiers. So when they could go no further, it was interesting to see what they would do; for they would sit down and say their prayers, sitting on an old saddle, or their knapsacks, maybe, and then take off their boots and their stockings, and lean their chin on the barrel of their musket. Then they would put their toe on the trigger, and *pouf!* it was all over, and there was no more marching for those fine old Grenadiers. Oh, it was very rough work up there on these Guadarama mountains!'

'And what army was this?' I asked.

'Oh, I have served in so many armies that I mix them up sometimes. Yes, I have seen much of war. Apropos I have seen your Scotchmen fight, and very stout *fantassins* they make, but I thought from them, that the folk over here all wore — how do you say it? — petticoats.'

'Those are the kilts, and they wear them only in the Highlands.'

'Ah! on the mountains. But there is a man

out yonder. Maybe he is the one who your father said would carry my letters to the post.'

'Yes, he is Farmer Whitehead's man. Shall I give them to him?'

'Well, he would be more careful of them if he had them from your hand.'

He took them from his pocket and gave them over to me. I hurried out with them, and as I did so my eyes fell upon the address of the topmost one. It was written very large and clear:

A SON MAJESTE,
LE ROI DE SUEDE,
STOCKHOLM.

I did not know very much French, but I had enough to make that out. What sort of eagle was this which had flown into our humble little nest?

7

The Corriemuir Peel Tower

Well, it would weary me, and I am very sure that it would weary you also, if I were to attempt to tell you how life went with us after this man came under our roof, or the way in which he gradually came to win the affections of every one of us. With the women it was quick work enough; but soon he had thawed my father too, which was no such easy matter, and had gained Jim Horscroft's goodwill as well as my own. Indeed, we were but two great boys beside him, for he had been everywhere and seen everything; and of an evening he would chatter away in his limping English until he took us clean from the plain kitchen and the little farm steading, to plunge us into courts and camps and battlefields and all the wonders of the world. Horscroft had been sulky enough with him at first; but de Lapp, with his tact and his easy ways, soon drew him round, until he had quite won his heart, and Jim would sit with Cousin Edie's hand in his, and the two be quite lost in listening to all that he had to tell us. I will not tell you all this; but even now, after so long an interval, I can trace how, week by week and month by month, by this word and that deed, he moulded us all as he wished.

One of his first acts was to give my father the boat in which he had come, reserving only the right to have it back in case he should have need of it. The herring were down on the coast that autumn, and my uncle before he died had given us a fine set of nets, so the gift was worth many a pound to us. Sometimes de Lapp would go out in the boat alone, and I have seen him for a whole summer day rowing slowly along and stopping every half-dozen strokes to throw over a stone at the end of a string. I could not think what he was doing until he told me of his own freewill.

'I am fond of studying all that has to do with the military,' said he, 'and I never lose a chance. I was wondering if it would be a difficult matter for the commander of an army corps to throw his men ashore here.'

'If the wind were not from the east,' said I.

'Ah! quite so, if the wind were not from the east. Have you taken soundings here?'

'No.'

'Your line of battleships would have to lie outside; but there is water enough for a forty-gun frigate right up within musket range. Cram your boats with *tirailleurs*, deploy them behind these sandhills, then back with the launches for more, and a stream of grape over their heads from the frigates. It could be done! It could be done!'

His moustaches bristled out more like a cat's than ever, and I could see by the flash of his eyes that he was carried away by his dream.

'You forget that our soldiers would be upon the beach,' said I indignantly.

'Ta, ta, ta!' he cried. 'Of course it takes two sides to make a battle. Let us see now; let us work it out. What could you get together? Shall we say twenty, thirty thousand. A few regiments of good troops: the rest, *pouf!* — conscripts, *bourgeois* with arms. How do you call them — volunteers?'

'Brave men!' I shouted.

'Oh yes, very brave men, but imbecile. Ah, *mon Dieu*, it is incredible how imbecile they would be! Not they alone, I mean, but all young troops. They are so afraid of being afraid that they would take no precaution. Ah, I have seen it! In Spain I have seen a battalion of conscripts attack a battery of ten pieces. Up they went, ah, so gallantly! and presently the hillside looked, from where I stood, like — how do you say it in English?

— a raspberry tart. And where was our fine battalion of conscripts? Then another battalion of young troops tried it, all together in a rush, shouting and yelling; but what will shouting do against a *mitraille* of grape? And there was our second battalion laid out on the hillside. And then the foot *chasseurs* of the Guard, old soldiers, were told to take the battery; and there was nothing fine about their advance — no column, no shouting, nobody killed — just a few scattered lines of *tirailleurs* and *pelotons* of support; but in ten minutes the guns were silenced, and the Spanish gunners cut to pieces. War must be learned, my young friend, just the same as the farming of sheep.'

'Pooh!' said I, not to be out-crowed by a foreigner. 'If we had thirty thousand men on the line of the hill yonder, you would come to be very glad that you had your boats behind you.'

'On the line of the hill?' said he, with a flash of his eyes along the ridge. 'Yes, if your man knew his business he would have his left about your house, his centre on Corriemuir, and his right over near the doctor's house, with his *tirailleurs* pushed out thickly in front. His horse, of course, would try to cut us up as we deployed on the beach. But once let us form, and we should soon know what to do.

81

There's the weak point, there at the gap. I would sweep it with my guns, then roll in my cavalry, push the infantry on in grand columns, and that wing would find itself up in the air. Eh, Jack, where would your volunteers be?'

'Close at the heels of your hindmost man,' said I; and we both burst out into the hearty laugh with which such discussions usually ended.

Sometimes when he talked I thought he was joking, and at other times it was not quite so easy to say. I well remember one evening that summer, when he was sitting in the kitchen with my father, Jim, and me, after the women had gone to bed, he began about Scotland and its relation to England.

'You used to have your own king and your own laws made at Edinburgh,' said he. 'Does it not fill you with rage and despair when you think that it all comes to you from London now?'

Jim took his pipe out of his mouth.

'It was we who put our king over the English; so if there's any rage, it should have been over yonder,' said he.

This was clearly news to the stranger, and it silenced him for the moment.

'Well, but your laws are made down there, and surely that is not good,' he said at last.

'No, it would be well to have a Parliament back in Edinburgh,' said my father; 'but I am kept so busy with the sheep that I have little enough time to think of such things.'

'It is for fine young men like you two to think of it,' said de Lapp. 'When a country is injured, it is to its young men that it looks to avenge it.'

'Aye! the English take too much upon themselves sometimes,' said Jim.

'Well, if there are many of that way of thinking about, why should we not form them into battalions and march them upon London?' cried de Lapp.

'That would be a rare little picnic,' said I, laughing. 'And who would lead us?'

He jumped up, bowing, with his hand on his heart, in his queer fashion.

'If you will allow me to have the honour!' he cried; and then seeing that we were all laughing, he began to laugh also, but I am sure that there was really no thought of a joke in his mind.

I could never make out what his age could be, nor could Jim Horscroft either. Sometimes we thought that he was an oldish man that looked young, and at others that he was a youngish man who looked old. His brown, stiff, close-cropped hair needed no cropping at the top, where it thinned away to a shining curve. His skin too was intersected by a thousand fine wrinkles, lacing and interlacing, and was all burned, as I have already said, by the sun. Yet he was as lithe as a boy, and he was as tough as whalebone, walking all day over the hills or rowing on the sea without turning a hair. On the whole we thought that he might be about forty or forty-five, though it was hard to see how he could have seen so much of life in the time. But one day we got talking of ages, and then he surprised us.

I had been saying that I was just twenty, and Jim said that he was twenty-seven.

'Then I am the most old of the three,' said de Lapp.

We laughed at this, for by our reckoning he might almost have been our father.

'But not by so much,' said he, arching his brows. 'I was nine-and-twenty in December.'

And it was this even more than his talk which made us understand what an extraordinary life it must have been that he had led. He saw our astonishment, and laughed at it.

'I have lived! I have lived!' he cried. 'I have spent my days and my nights. I led a company in a battle where five nations were engaged when I was but fourteen. I made a king turn pale at the words I whispered in his ear when I was twenty. I had a hand in

84

remaking a kingdom and putting a fresh king upon a great throne the very year that I came of age. *Mon Dieu*, I have lived my life!'

That was the most that I ever heard him confess of his past life, and he only shook his head and laughed when we tried to get something more out of him. There were times when we thought that he was but a clever impostor; for what could a man of such influence and talents be loitering here in Berwickshire for? But one day there came an incident which showed us that he had indeed a history in the past.

You will remember that there was an old officer of the Peninsula who lived no great way from us, the same who danced round the bonfire with his sister and the two maids. He had gone up to London on some business about his pension and his wound money, and the chance of having some work given him, so that he did not come back until late in the autumn. One of the first days after his return he came down to see us, and there for the first time he clapped eyes upon de Lapp. Never in my life did I look upon so astonished a face, and he stared at our friend for a long minute without so much as a word. De Lapp looked back at him equally hard, but there was no recognition in his eyes.

'I do not know who you are, sir,' he said at

last; 'but you look at me as if you had seen me before.'

'So I have,' answered the Major.

'Never to my knowledge.'

'But I'll swear it!'

'Where then?'

'At the village of Astorga, in the year '08.'

De Lapp started, and stared again at our neighbour.

'*Mon Dieu*, what a chance!' he cried. 'And you were the English *parlementaire*? I remember you very well indeed, sir. Let me have a whisper in your ear.'

He took him aside and talked very earnestly with him in French for a quarter of an hour, gesticulating with his hands, and explaining something, while the Major nodded his old grizzled head from time to time. At last they seemed to come to some agreement, and I heard the Major say '*Parole d'honneur*' several times, and afterwards '*Fortune de la guerre*,' which I could very well understand, for they gave you a fine upbringing at Birtwhistle's. But after that I always noticed that the Major never used the same free fashion of speech that we did towards our lodger, but bowed when he addressed him, and treated him with a wonderful deal of respect. I asked the Major more than once what he knew about him, but he always put it off, and I could get no answer out of him.

Jim Horscroft was at home all that summer, but late in the autumn he went back to Edinburgh again for the winter session, and as he intended to work very hard and get his degree next spring if he could, he said that he would bide up there for the Christmas. So there was a great leave-taking between him and Cousin Edie; and he was to put up his plate and to marry her as soon as he had the right to practise. I never knew a man love a woman more fondly than he did her, and she liked him well enough in a way — for, indeed, in the whole of Scotland she would not find a finer looking man — but when it came to marriage, I think she winced a little at the thought that all her wonderful dreams should end in nothing more than in being the wife of a country surgeon. Still there was only me and Jim to choose out of, and she took the best of us.

Of course there was de Lapp also; but we always felt that he was of an altogether different class to us, and so he didn't count. I was never very sure at that time whether Edie cared for him or not. When Jim was at home they took little notice of each other. After he was gone they were thrown more together, which was natural enough, as he had taken up so much of her time before. Once or twice she spoke to me about de Lapp as though she did not like him, and yet she was uneasy if he were not in in the evening; and there was no one so fond of his talk, or with so many questions to ask him, as she. She made him describe what queens wore, and what sort of carpets they walked on, and whether they had hairpins in their hair, and how many feathers they had in their hats, until it was a wonder to me how he could find an answer to it all. And yet an answer he always had; and was so ready and quick with his tongue, and so anxious to amuse her, that I wondered how it was that she did not like him better.

Well, the summer and the autumn and the best part of the winter passed away, and we were still all very happy together. We got well into the year 1815, and the great Emperor was still eating his heart out at Elba; and all the ambassadors were wrangling together at Vienna as to what they should do with the lion's skin, now that they had so fairly hunted him down. And we in our little corner of Europe went on with our petty peaceful business, looking after the sheep, attending the Berwick cattle fairs, and chatting at night round the blazing peat fire. We never thought that what all these high and mighty people were doing could have any bearing upon us;

and as to war, why everybody was agreed that the great shadow was lifted from us for ever, and that, unless the Allies quarrelled among themselves, there would not be a shot fired in Europe for another fifty years.

There was one incident, however, that stands out very clearly in my memory. I think that it must have happened about the February of this year, and I will tell it to you before I go any further.

You know what the border peel castles are like, I have no doubt. They were just square heaps built every here and there along the line, so that the folk might have some place of protection against raiders and mosstroopers. When Percy and his men were over the Marches, then the people would drive some of their cattle into the yard of the tower, shut up the big gate, and light a fire in the brazier at the top, which would be answered by all the other peel towers, until the lights would go twinkling up to the Lammermuir Hills, and so carry the news on to the Pentlands and to Edinburgh. But now, of course, all these old keeps were warped and crumbling, and made fine nesting places for the wild birds. Many a good egg have I had for my collection out of the Corriemuir Peel Tower.

One day I had been a very long walk, away over to leave a message at the Laidlaw

Armstrongs, who live two miles on this side of Ayton. About five o'clock, just before the sun set, I found myself on the brae path with the gable end of West Inch peeping up in front of me and the old peel tower lying on my left. I turned my eyes on the keep, for it looked so fine with the flush of the level sun beating full upon it and the blue sea stretching out behind; and as I stared, I suddenly saw the face of a man twinkle for a moment in one of the holes in the wall.

Well I stood and wondered over this, for what could anybody be doing in such a place now that it was too early for the nesting season? It was so queer that I was determined to come to the bottom of it; so, tired as I was, I turned my shoulder on home, and walked swiftly towards the tower. The grass stretches right up to the very base of the wall, and my feet made little noise until I reached the crumbling arch where the old gate used to be. I peeped through, and there was Bonaventure de Lapp standing inside the keep, and peeping out through the very hole at which I had seen his face. He was turned half away from me, and it was clear that he had not seen me at all, for he was staring with all his eyes over in the direction of West Inch. As I advanced my foot rattled the rubble that lay in the gateway, and he turned round with a start and faced me.

He was not a man whom you could put out of countenance, and his face changed no more than if he had been expecting me there for a twelvemonth; but there was something in his eyes which let me know that he would have paid a good price to have me back on the brae path again.

'Hullo!' said I, 'what are you doing here?'

'I may ask you that,' said he.

'I came up because I saw your face at the window.'

'And I because, as you may well have observed, I have very much interest for all that has to do with the military, and, of course, castles are among them. You will excuse me for one moment, my dear Jack.'

And he stepped out suddenly through the hole in the wall, so as to be out of my sight.

But I was very much too curious to excuse him so easily. I shifted my ground swiftly to see what it was that he was after. He was standing outside, and waving his hand frantically, as in a signal.

'What are you doing?' I cried; and then, running out to his side, I looked across the moors to see whom he was beckoning to.

'You go too far, sir,' said he, angrily; 'I didn't thought you would have gone so far. A gentleman has the freedom to act as he

91

choose without your being the spy upon him. If we are to be friends, you must not interfere in my affairs.'

'I don't like these secret doings,' said I, 'and my father would not like them either.'

'Your father can speak for himself, and there is no secret,' said he, curtly. 'It is you with your imaginings that make a secret. Ta, ta, ta! I have no patience with such foolishness.'

And without as much as a nod, he turned his back upon me, and started walking swiftly to West Inch.

Well, I followed him, and in the worst of tempers; for I had a feeling that there was some mischief in the wind, and yet I could not for the life of me think what it all meant. Again I found myself puzzling over the whole mystery of this man's coming, and of his long residence among us. And whom could he have expected to meet at the peel tower? Was the fellow a spy, and was it some brother spy who came to speak with him there? But that was absurd. What could there be to spy about in Berwickshire? And besides, Major Elliott knew all about him, and he would not show him such respect if there were anything amiss.

I had just got as far as this in my thoughts when I heard a cheery hail, and there was the Major himself coming down the hill from his house, with his big bulldog Bounder held in leash. This dog was a savage creature, and had caused more than one accident on the countryside; but the Major was very fond of it, and would never go out without it, though he kept it tied with a good thick thong of leather. Well, just as I was looking at the Major, waiting for him to come up, he stumbled with his lame leg over a branch of gorse, and in recovering himself he let go his hold of the leash, and in an instant there was the beast of a dog flying down the hillside in my direction.

I did not like it, I can tell you; for there was neither stick nor stone about, and I knew that the brute was dangerous. The Major was shrieking to it from behind, and I think that the creature thought that he was hallooing it on, so furiously did it rush. But I knew its name, and I thought that maybe that might give me the privileges of acquaintanceship; so as it came at me with bristling hair and its nose screwed back between its two red eyes, I cried out 'Bounder! Bounder!' at the pitch of my lungs. It had its effect, for the beast passed me with a snarl, and flew along the path on the traces of Bonaventure de Lapp.

He turned at the shouting, and seemed to take in the whole thing at a glance; but he strolled along as slowly as ever. My heart was in my mouth for him, for the dog had never seen him before; and I ran as fast as my feet would carry me to drag it away from him. But somehow, as it bounded up and saw the twittering finger and thumb which de Lapp held out behind him, its fury died suddenly away, and we saw it wagging its thumb of a tail and clawing at his knee.

'Your dog then, Major?' said he, as its owner came hobbling up. 'Ah, it is a fine beast — a fine, pretty thing!'

The Major was blowing hard, for he had covered the ground nearly as fast as I.

'I was afraid lest he might have hurt you,' he panted.

'Ta, ta, ta!' cried de Lapp. 'He is a pretty, gentle thing; I always love the dogs. But I am glad that I have met you, Major; for here is this young gentleman, to whom I owe very much, who has begun to think that I am a spy. Is it not so, Jack?'

I was so taken aback by his words that I could not lay my tongue to an answer, but coloured up and looked askance, like the awkward country lad that I was.

'You know me, Major,' said de Lapp, 'and I am sure that you will tell him that this could not be.'

'No, no, Jack! Certainly not! Certainly not!' cried the Major.

'Thank you,' said de Lapp. 'You know me, and you do me justice. And yourself, I hope that your knee is better, and that you will soon have your regiment given you.'

'I am well enough,' answered the Major; 'but they will never give me a place unless there is war, and there will be no more war in my time.'

'Oh, you think that!' said de Lapp with a smile. 'Well, *nous verrons!* We shall see, my friend!'

He whisked off his hat, and turning briskly he walked off in the direction of West Inch. The Major stood looking after him with thoughtful eyes, and then asked me what it was that had made me think that he was a spy. When I told him he said nothing, but he shook his head, and looked like a man who was ill at ease in his mind.

8

The Coming of the Cutter

I never felt quite the same to our lodger after that little business at the peel castle. It was always in my mind that he was holding a secret from me — indeed, that he was all a secret together, seeing that he always hung a veil over his past. And when by chance that veil was for an instant whisked away, we always caught just a glimpse of something bloody and violent and dreadful upon the other side. The very look of his body was terrible. I bathed with him once in the summer, and I saw then that he was haggled with wounds all over. Besides seven or eight scars and slashes, his ribs on one side were all twisted out of shape, and a part of one of his calves had been torn away. He laughed in his merry way when he saw my face of wonder.

'Cossacks! Cossacks!' said he, running his hand over his scars. 'And the ribs were broke by an artillery tumbril. It is very bad to have the guns pass over one. Now with cavalry it is nothing. A horse will pick its steps however fast it may go. I have been ridden over by fifteen hundred cuirassiers and by the Russian hussars of Grodno, and I had no harm from that. But guns are very bad.'

'And the calf?' I asked.

'*Pouf!* It is only a wolf bite,' said he. 'You would not think how I came by it! You will understand that my horse and I had been struck, the horse killed, and I with my ribs broken by the tumbril. Well, it was cold — oh, bitter, bitter! — the ground like iron, and no one to help the wounded, so that they froze into such shapes as would make you smile. I too felt that I was freezing, so what did I do? I took my sword, and I opened my dead horse, so well as I could, and I made space in him for me to lie, with one little hole for my mouth. *Sapristi!* It was warm enough there. But there was not room for the entire of me, so my feet and part of my legs stuck out. Then in the night, when I slept, there came the wolves to eat the horse, and they had a little pinch of me also, as you can see; but after that I was on guard with my pistols, and they had no more of me. There I lived, very warm and nice, for ten days.'

'Ten days!' I cried. 'What did you eat?'

'Why, I ate the horse. It was what you call board and lodging to me. But of course I have sense to eat the legs, and live in the body. There were many dead about who had all their water bottles, so I had all I could wish. And on the eleventh day there came a patrol of light cavalry, and all was well.'

It was by such chance chats as these — hardly worth repeating in themselves — that there came light upon himself and his past. But the day was coming when we should know all; and how it came I shall try now to tell you.

The winter had been a dreary one, but with March came the first signs of spring, and for a week on end we had sunshine and winds from the south. On the 7th Jim Horscroft was to come back from Edinburgh; for though the session ended with the 1st, his examination would take him a week. Edie and I were out walking on the sea beach on the 6th, and I could talk of nothing but my old friend — for, indeed, he was the only friend of my own age that I had at that time. Edie was very silent, which was a rare thing with her; but she listened smiling to all that I had to say.

'Poor old Jim!' said she once or twice under her breath. 'Poor old Jim!'

'And if he has passed,' said I, 'why, then of course he will put up his plate and have his own house, and we shall be losing our Edie.'

I tried to make a jest of it and to speak lightly, but the words still stuck in my throat.

'Poor old Jim!' said she again, and there

were tears in her eyes as she said it. 'And poor old Jock!' she added, slipping her hand into mine as we walked. 'You cared for me a little bit once also, didn't you, Jock? Oh, is not that a sweet little ship out yonder!'

It was a dainty cutter of about thirty tons, very swift by the rake of her masts and the lines of her bow. She was coming up from the south under jib, foresail, and mainsail; but even as we watched her all her white canvas shut suddenly in, like a kittiwake closing her wings, and we saw the splash of her anchor just under her bowsprit. She may have been rather less than a quarter of a mile from the shore — so near that I could see a tall man with a peaked cap, who stood at the quarter with a telescope to his eye, sweeping it backwards and forwards along the coast.

'What can they want here?' asked Edie.

'They are rich English from London,' said I; for that was how we explained everything that was above our comprehension in the border counties. We stood for the best part of an hour watching the bonny craft, and then, as the sun was lying low on a cloudbank and there was a nip in the evening air, we turned back to West Inch.

As you come to the farmhouse from the front, you pass up a garden, with little enough in it, which leads out by a wicket-gate to the

road; the same gate at which we stood on the
night when the beacons were lit, the night
that we saw Walter Scott ride past on his way
to Edinburgh. On the right of this gate, on
the garden side, was a bit of a rockery which
was said to have been made by my father's
mother many years before. She had fashioned
it out of water-worn stones and sea shells,
with mosses and ferns in the chinks. Well, as
we came in through the gates my eyes fell
upon this stone heap, and there was a letter
stuck in a cleft stick upon the top of it. I took
a step forward to see what it was, but Edie
sprang in front of me, and plucking it off she
thrust it into her pocket.

'That's for me,' said she, laughing. But I
stood looking at her with a face which drove
the laugh from her lips.

'Who is it from, Edie?' I asked.

She pouted, but made no answer.

'Who is it from, woman?' I cried. 'Is it
possible that you have been as false to Jim as
you were to me?'

'How rude you are, Jock!' she cried. 'I do
wish that you would mind your own business.'

'There is only one person that it could be
from,' I cried. 'It is from this man de Lapp!'

'And suppose that you are right, Jock?'

The coolness of the woman amazed and
enraged me.

'You confess it!' I cried. 'Have you, then, no shame left?'

'Why should I not receive letters from this gentleman?'

'Because it is infamous.'

'And why?'

'Because he is a stranger.'

'On the contrary,' said she, 'he is my husband!'

9

The Doings at West Inch

I can remember that moment so well. I have heard from others that a great, sudden blow has dulled their senses. It was not so with me. On the contrary, I saw and heard and thought more clearly than I had ever done before. I can remember that my eyes caught a little knob of marble as broad as my palm, which was imbedded in one of the grey stones of the rockery, and I found time to admire its delicate mottling. And yet the look upon my face must have been strange, for Cousin Edie screamed, and leaving me she ran off to the house. I followed her and tapped at the window of her room, for I could see that she was there.

'Go away, Jock, go away!' she cried. 'You are going to scold me! I won't be scolded! I won't open the window! Go away!'

But I continued to tap.

'I must have a word with you!'

'What is it, then?' she cried, raising the sash about three inches. 'The moment you begin to scold I shall close it.'

102

'Are you really married, Edie?'

'Yes, I am married.'

'Who married you?'

'Father Brennan, at the Roman Catholic Chapel at Berwick.'

'And you a Presbyterian?'

'He wished it to be in a Catholic Church.'

'When was it?'

'On Wednesday week.'

I remembered then that on that day she had driven over to Berwick, while de Lapp had been away on a long walk, as he said, among the hills.

'What about Jim?' I asked.

'Oh, Jim will forgive me!'

'You will break his heart and ruin his life.'

'No, no; he will forgive me.'

'He will murder de Lapp! Oh, Edie, how could you bring such disgrace and misery upon us?'

'Ah, now you are scolding!' she cried, and down came the window.

I waited some little time, and tapped, for I had much still to ask her; but she would return no answer, and I thought that I could hear her sobbing. At last I gave it up; and I was about to go into the house, for it was nearly dark now, when I heard the click of the garden gate. It was de Lapp himself.

But as he came up the path he seemed to

me to be either mad or drunk. He danced as he walked, cracked his fingers in the air, and his eyes blazed like two will-o'-the-wisps. '*Voltigeurs!*' he shouted; '*Voltigeurs de la Garde!*' just as he had done when he was off his head; and then suddenly, '*En avant! En avant!*' and up he came, waving his walking-cane over his head. He stopped short when he saw me looking at him, and I daresay he felt a bit ashamed of himself.

'Hola, Jock!' he cried. 'I didn't thought anybody was there. I am in what you call the high spirits to-night.'

'So it seems!' said I, in my blunt fashion. 'You may not feel so merry when my friend Jim Horscroft comes back to-morrow.'

'Ah! he comes back to-morrow, does he? And why should I not feel merry?'

'Because, if I know the man, he will kill you.'

'Ta, ta, ta!' cried de Lapp. 'I see that you know of our marriage. Edie has told you. Jim may do what he likes.'

'You have given us a nice return for having taken you in.'

'My good fellow,' said he, 'I have, as you say, given you a very nice return. I have taken Edie from a life which is unworthy of her, and I have connected you by marriage with a noble family. However, I have some letters which I must write to-night, and the rest we can talk over to-morrow, when your friend Jim is here to help us.'

He stepped towards the door.

'And this was whom you were awaiting at the peel tower!' I cried, seeing light suddenly.

'Why, Jock, you are becoming quite sharp,' said he, in a mocking tone; and an instant later I heard the door of his room close and the key turn in the lock.

I thought that I should see him no more that night; but a few minutes later he came into the kitchen, where I was sitting with the old folk.

'Madame,' said he, bowing down with his hand over his heart, in his own queer fashion, 'I have met with much kindness in your hands, and it shall always be in my heart. I didn't thought I could have been so happy in the quiet country as you have made me. You will accept this small souvenir; and you also, sir, you will take this little gift, which I have the honour to make to you.'

He put two little paper packets down upon the table at their elbows, and then, with three more bows to my mother, he walked from the room.

Her present was a brooch, with a green stone set in the middle and a dozen little shining white ones all round it. We had never seen such things before, and did not know how to set a name to them; but they told us afterwards at Berwick that the big one was an emerald and the others were diamonds, and that they were worth much more than all the lambs we had that spring. My dear old mother has been gone now this many a year, but that bonny brooch sparkles at the neck of my eldest daughter when she goes out into company; and I never look at it that I do not see the keen eyes and the long thin nose and the cat's whiskers of our lodger at West Inch. As to my father, he had a fine gold watch with a double case; and a proud man was he as he sat with it in the palm of his hand, his ear stooping to hearken to the tick. I do not know which was best pleased, and they would talk of nothing but what de Lapp had given them.

'He's given you something more,' said I at last.

'What then, Jock?' asked father.

'A husband for Cousin Edie,' said I.

They thought I was daffing when I said that; but when they came to understand that it was the real truth, they were as proud and as pleased as if I had told them that she had married the laird. Indeed, poor Jim, with his hard drinking and his fighting, had not a very bright name on the country-side, and my mother had often said that no good could come of such a match. Now, de Lapp was, for all we knew, steady and quiet and well-to-do. And as to the secrecy of it, secret marriages were very common in Scotland at that time, when only a few words were needed to make man and wife, so nobody thought much of that. The old folk were as pleased, then, as if their rent had been lowered; but I was still sore at heart, for it seemed to me that my friend had been cruelly dealt with, and I knew well that he was not a man who would easily put up with it.

10

The Return of the Shadow

I woke with a heavy heart the next morning, for I knew that Jim would be home before long, and that it would be a day of trouble. But how much trouble that day was to bring, or how far it would alter the lives of us, was more than I had ever thought in my darkest moments. But let me tell you it all, just in the order that it happened.

I had to get up early that morning; for it was just the first flush of the lambing, and my father and I were out on the moors as soon as it was fairly light. As I came out into the passage a wind struck upon my face, and there was the house door wide open, and the grey light drawing another door upon the inner wall. And when I looked again there was Edie's room open also, and de Lapp's too; and I saw in a flash what that giving of presents meant upon the evening before. It was a leave-taking, and they were gone.

My heart was bitter against Cousin Edie as I stood looking into her room. To think that for the sake of a newcomer she could leave us all without one kindly word, or as much as a handshake. And he, too! I had been afraid of what would happen when Jim met him; but now there seemed to be something cowardly in this avoidance of him. I was angry and hurt and sore, and I went out into the open without a word to my father, and climbed up on to the moors to cool my flushed face.

When I got up to Corriemuir I caught my last glimpse of Cousin Edie. The little cutter still lay where she had anchored, but a rowboat was pulling out to her from the shore. In the stern I saw a flutter of red, and I knew that it came from her shawl. I watched the boat reach the yacht and the folk climb on to her deck. Then the anchor came up, the white wings spread once more, and away she dipped right out to sea. I still saw that little red spot on the deck, and de Lapp standing beside her. They could see me also, for I was outlined against the sky, and they both waved their hands for a long time, but gave it up at last when they found that I would give them no answer.

I stood with my arms folded, feeling as glum as ever I did in my life, until their cutter was only a square hickering patch of white among the mists of the morning. It was breakfast time and the porridge upon the table before I got back, but I had no heart for the food. The old folk had taken the matter coolly enough, though my mother had no word too hard for Edie; for the two had never had much love for each other, and less of late than ever.

'There's a letter here from him,' said my father, pointing to a note folded up on the table; 'it was in his room. Maybe you would read it to us.'

They had not even opened it; for, truth to tell, neither of the good folk were very clever at reading ink, though they could do well with a fine large print.

It was addressed in big letters to 'The good people of West Inch' and this was the note, which lies before me all stained and faded as I write:

My friends, — I didn't thought to have left you so suddenly, but the matter was in other hands than mine. Duty and honour have called me back to my old comrades. This you will doubtless understand before many days are past. I take your Edie with me as my wife; and it may be that in some more peaceful time you will see us again at West Inch. Meanwhile, accept the assurance of my affection, and believe me that I shall never forget the quiet months which I spent with you, at the time when my life would have been worth a week at the utmost had I been taken by the Allies. But the reason of this you may also learn some day.

Yours,

BONAVENTURE DE LISSAC
(Colonel des Voltigeurs de la Garde, et aide-de-camp de S.M.I. L'Empereur Napoleon.)

I whistled when I came to those words written under his name; for though I had long made up my mind that our lodger could be none other than one of those wonderful soldiers of whom we had heard so much, who had forced their way into every capital of Europe, save only our own, still I had little thought that our roof covered Napoleon's own aide-de-camp and a colonel of his Guard.

'So,' said I, 'de Lissac is his name, and not de Lapp. Well, colonel or no, it is as well for him that he got away from here before Jim laid hands upon him. And time enough, too,' I added, peeping out at the kitchen window, 'for here is the man himself coming through the garden.'

I ran to the door to meet him, feeling that I would have given a deal to have him back in

Edinburgh again. He came running, waving a paper over his head; and I thought that maybe he had a note from Edie, and that it was all known to him. But as he came up I saw that it was a big, stiff, yellow paper which crackled as he waved it, and that his eyes were dancing with happiness.

'Hurrah, Jock!' he shouted. 'Where is Edie? Where is Edie?'

'What is it, man?' I asked.

'Where is Edie?'

'What have you there?'

'It's my diploma, Jock. I can practise when I like. It's all right. I want to show it to Edie.'

'The best you can do is to forget all about Edie,' said I.

Never have I seen a man's face change as his did when I said those words.

'What! What d'ye mean, Jock Calder?' he stammered.

He let go his hold of the precious diploma as he spoke, and away it went over the hedge and across the moor, where it stuck flapping on a whin-bush; but he never so much as glanced at it. His eyes were bent upon me, and I saw the devil's spark glimmer up in the depths of them.

'She is not worthy of you,' said I.

He gripped me by the shoulder.

'What have you done?' he whispered. 'This

112

is some of your hanky-panky! Where is she?'

'She's off with that Frenchman who lodged here.'

I had been casting about in my mind how I could break it gently to him; but I was always backward in speech, and I could think of nothing better than this.

'Oh!' said he, and stood nodding his head and looking at me, though I knew very well that he could neither see me, nor the steading, nor anything else. So he stood for a minute or more, with his hands clenched and his head still nodding. Then he gave a gulp in his throat, and spoke in a queer dry, rasping voice.

'When was this?' said he.

'This morning.'

'Were they married?'

'Yes.'

He put his hand against the door-post to steady himself.

'Any message for me?'

'She said that you would forgive her.'

'May God blast my soul on the day I do! Where have they gone to?'

'To France, I should judge.'

'His name was de Lapp, I think?'

'His real name is de Lissac; and he is no less than a colonel in Boney's Guards.'

'Ah! he would be in Paris, likely. That is

well! That is well!'

'Hold up!' I shouted. 'Father! Father! Bring the brandy!'

His knees had given way for an instant, but he was himself again before the old man came running with the bottle.

'Take it away!' said he.

'Have a soop, Mister Horscroft,' cried my father, pressing it upon him. 'It will give you fresh heart!'

He caught hold of the bottle and sent it flying over the garden hedge.

'It's very good for those who wish to forget,' said he; 'I am going to remember!'

'May God forgive you for sinfu' waste!' cried my father aloud.

'And for well-nigh braining an officer of his Majesty's infantry!' said old Major Elliott, putting his head over the hedge. 'I could have done with a nip after a morning's walk, but it is something new to have a whole bottle whizz past my ear. But what is amiss, that you all stand round like mutes at a burying?'

In a few words I told him our trouble, while Jim, with a grey face and his brows drawn down, stood leaning against the door-post. The Major was as glum as we by the time I had finished, for he was fond both of Jim and of Edie.

'Tut, tut!' said he. 'I feared something of

114

the kind ever since that business of the peel tower. It's the way with the French. They can't leave the women alone. But, at least, de Lissac has married her, and that's a comfort. But it's no time now to think of our own little troubles, with all Europe in a roar again, and another twenty years' war before us, as like as not.'

'What d'ye mean?' I asked.

'Why, man, Napoleon's back from Elba, his troops have flocked to him, and Louis has run for his life. The news was in Berwick this morning.'

'Great Lord!' cried my father. 'Then the weary business is all to do over again!'

'Aye, we thought we were out from the shadow, but it's still there. Wellington is ordered from Vienna to the Low Countries, and it is thought that the Emperor will break out first on that side. Well, it's a bad wind that blows nobody any good. I've just had news that I am to join the 71st as senior major.'

I shook hands with our good neighbour on this, for I knew how it had lain upon his mind that he should be a cripple, with no part to play in the world.

'I am to join my regiment as soon as I can; and we shall be over yonder in a month, and in Paris, maybe, before another one is over.'

'By the Lord, then, I'm with you, Major!'

cried Jim Horscroft. 'I'm not too proud to carry a musket, if you will put me in front of this Frenchman.'

'My lad, I'd be proud to have you serve under me,' said the Major. 'And as to de Lissac, where the Emperor is he will be.'

'You know the man,' said I. 'What can you tell us of him?'

'There is no better officer in the French army, and that is a big word to say. They say that he would have been a marshal, but he preferred to stay at the Emperor's elbow. I met him two days before Corunna, when I was sent with a flag to speak about our wounded. He was with Soult then. I knew him again when I saw him.'

'And I will know him again when I see him!' said Horscroft, with the old dour look on his face.

And then at that instant, as I stood there, it was suddenly driven home to me how poor and purposeless a life I should lead while this crippled friend of ours and the companion of my boyhood were away in the forefront of the storm. Quick as a flash my resolution was taken.

'I'll come with you too, Major,' I cried.

'Jock! Jock!' said my father, wringing his hands.

Jim said nothing, but put his arm half

round me and hugged me. The Major's eyes shone and he flourished his cane in the air.

'My word, but I shall have two good recruits at my heels,' said he. 'Well, there's no time to be lost, so you must both be ready for the evening coach.'

And this was what a single day brought about; and yet years pass away so often without a change. Just think of the alteration in that four-and-twenty hours. De Lissac was gone. Edie was gone. Napoleon had escaped. War had broken out. Jim Horscroft had lost everything, and he and I were setting out to fight against the French. It was all like a dream, until I tramped off to the coach that evening, and looked back at the grey farm steading and at the two little dark figures: my mother with her face sunk in her Shetland shawl, and my father waving his drover's stick to hearten me upon my way.

11

The Gathering of the Nations

And now I come to a bit of my story that clean takes my breath away as I think of it, and makes me wish that I had never taken the job of telling it in hand. For when I write I like things to come slow and orderly and in their turn, like sheep coming out of a paddock. So it was at West Inch. But now that we were drawn into a larger life, like wee bits of straw that float slowly down some lazy ditch, until they suddenly find themselves in the dash and swirl of a great river; then it is very hard for me with my simple words to keep pace with it all. But you can find the cause and reason of everything in the books about history, and so I shall just leave that alone and talk about what I saw with my own eyes and heard with my own ears.

The regiment to which our friend had been appointed was the 71st Highland Light Infantry, which wore the red coat and the trews, and had its depot in Glasgow town. There we went, all three, by coach: the Major in great spirits and full of stories about the

Duke and the Peninsula, while Jim sat in the corner with his lips set and his arms folded, and I knew that he killed de Lissac three times an hour in his heart. I could tell it by the sudden glint of his eyes and grip of his hand. As to me, I did not know whether to be glad or sorry; for home is home, and it is a weary thing, however you may brazen it out, to feel that half Scotland is between you and your mother.

We were in Glasgow next day, and the Major took us down to the depot, where a soldier with three stripes on his arm and a fistful of ribbons from his cap, showed every tooth he had in his head at the sight of Jim, and walked three times round him to have the view of him, as if he had been Carlisle Castle. Then he came over to me and punched me in the ribs and felt my muscle, and was nigh as pleased as with Jim.

'These are the sort, Major, these are the sort,' he kept saying. 'With a thousand of these we could stand up to Boney's best.'

'How do they run?' asked the Major.

'A poor show,' said he, 'but they may lick into shape. The best men have been drafted to America, and we are full of militiamen and recruities.'

'Tut, tut!' said the Major. 'We'll have old soldiers and good ones against us. Come to

119

me if you need any help, you two.'

And so with a nod he left us, and we began to understand that a Major who is your officer is a very different person from a Major who happens to be your neighbour in the country.

Well, well, why should I trouble you with these things? I could wear out a good quill-pen just writing about what we did, Jim and I, at the depot in Glasgow; and how we came to know our officers and our comrades, and how they came to know us. Soon came the news that the folk of Vienna, who had been cutting up Europe as if it had been a jigget of mutton, had flown back, each to his own country, and that every man and horse in their armies had their faces towards France. We heard of great reviews and musterings in Paris too, and then that Wellington was in the Low Countries, and that on us and on the Prussians would fall the first blow. The Government was shipping men over to him as fast as they could, and every port along the east coast was choked with guns and horses and stores. On the third of June we had our marching orders also, and on the same night we took ship from Leith, reaching Ostend the night after. It was my first sight of a foreign land, and indeed most of my comrades were the same, for we were very young in the ranks. I can see the blue waters now, and the curling surf line, and the long yellow beach, and queer windmills twisting and turning — a thing that a man would not see from one end of Scotland to the other. It was a clean, well-kept town, but the folk were undersized, and there was neither ale nor oatmeal cakes to be bought amongst them.

From there we went on to a place called Bruges; and from there to Ghent, where we picked up with the 52nd and the 95th, which were the two regiments that we were brigaded with. It's a wonderful place for churches and stonework is Ghent, and indeed of all the towns we were in there was scarce one but had a finer kirk than any in Glasgow. From there we pushed on to Ath, which is a little village on a river, or a burn rather, called the Dender. There we were quartered — in tents mostly, for it was fine sunny weather — and the whole brigade set to work at its drill from morning till evening. General Adams was our chief, and Reynell was our colonel, and they were both fine old soldiers; but what put heart into us most was to think that we were under the Duke, for his name was like a bugle call. He was at Brussels with the bulk of the army, but we knew that we should see him quick enough if he were needed.

I had never seen so many English together, and indeed I had a kind of contempt for them, as folk always have if they live near a border. But the two regiments that were with us now were as good comrades as could be wished. The 52nd had a thousand men in the ranks, and there were many old soldiers of the Peninsula among them. They came from Oxfordshire for the most part. The 95th were a rifle regiment, and had dark green coats instead of red. It was strange to see them loading, for they would put the ball into a greasy rag and then hammer it down with a mallet, but they could fire both further and straighter than we. All that part of Belgium was covered with British troops at that time; for the Guards were over near Enghien, and there were cavalry regiments on the further side of us. You see, it was very necessary that Wellington should spread out all his force, for Boney was behind the screen of his fortresses, and of course we had no means of saying on what side he might pop out, except that he was pretty sure to come the way that we least expected him. On the one side he might get between us and the sea, and so cut us off from England; and on the other he might shove in between the Prussians and ourselves. But the Duke was as clever as he, for he had his horse and his light troops all round him, like a great spider's web, so that the moment a French foot stepped across the border he could close up all his men at the right place.

For myself, I was very happy at Ath, and I found the folk very kindly and homely. There was a farmer of the name of Bois, in whose fields we were quartered, and who was a real good friend to many of us. We built him a wooden barn among us in our spare time, and many a time I and Jeb Seaton, my rear-rank man, have hung out his washing, for the smell of the wet linen seemed to take us both straight home as nothing else could do. I have often wondered whether that good man and his wife are still living, though I think it hardly likely, for they were of a hale middle-age at the time. Jim would come with us too, sometimes, and would sit with us smoking in the big Flemish kitchen, but he was a different Jim now to the old one. He had always had a hard touch in him, but now his trouble seemed to have turned him to flint, and I never saw a smile upon his face, and seldom heard a word from his lips. His whole mind was set on revenging himself upon de Lissac for having taken Edie from him, and he would sit for hours with his chin upon his hands glaring and frowning, all wrapped in the one idea. This made him a bit of a butt among the men at first, and they laughed at him for it; but when they came to know him better they found that he was not a good man to laugh at, and then they dropped it.

We were early risers at that time, and the whole brigade was usually under arms at the flush of dawn. One morning — it was the sixteenth of June — we had just formed up, and General Adams had ridden up to give some order to Colonel Reynell within a musket-length of where I stood, when suddenly they both stood staring along the Brussels road. None of us dared move our heads, but every eye in the regiment whisked round, and there we saw an officer with the cockade of a general's aide-de-camp thundering down the road as hard as a great dapple-grey horse could carry him. He bent his face over its mane and flogged at its neck with the slack of the bridle, as though he rode for very life.

'Hullo, Reynell!' says the general. 'This begins to look like business. What do you make of it?'

They both cantered their horses forward, and Adams tore open the dispatch which the messenger handed to him. The wrapper had not touched the ground before he turned, waving the letter over his head as if it had been a sabre.

'Dismiss!' he cried. 'General parade and

march in half-an-hour.'

Then in an instant all was buzz and bustle, and the news on every lip. Napoleon had crossed the frontier the day before, had pushed the Prussians before him, and was already deep in the country to the east of us with a hundred and fifty thousand men. Away we scuttled to gather our things together and have our breakfast, and in an hour we had marched off and left Ath and the Dender behind us for ever. There was good need for haste, for the Prussians had sent no news to Wellington of what was doing, and though he had rushed from Brussels at the first whisper of it, like a good old mastiff from its kennel, it was hard to see how he could come up in time to help the Prussians.

It was a bright warm morning, and as the brigade tramped down the broad Belgian road the dust rolled up from it like the smoke of a battery. I tell you that we blessed the man that planted the poplars along the sides, for their shadow was better than drink to us. Over across the fields, both to the right and the left, were other roads, one quite close, and the other a mile or more from us. A column of infantry was marching down the near one, and it was a fair race between us, for we were each walking for all we were worth. There was such a wreath of dust round them that we could only see the gun-barrels and the bearskins breaking out here and there, with the head and shoulders of a mounted officer coming out above the cloud, and the flutter of the colours. It was a brigade of the Guards, but we could not tell which, for we had two of them with us in the campaign. On the far road there was also dust and to spare, but through it there flashed every now and then a long twinkle of brightness, like a hundred silver beads threaded in a line; and the breeze brought down such a snarling, clanging, clashing kind of music as I had never listened to. If I had been left to myself it would have been long before I knew what it was; but our corporals and sergeants were all old soldiers, and I had one trudging along with his halbert at my elbow, who was full of precept and advice.

'That's heavy horse,' said he. 'You see that double twinkle? That means they have helmet as well as cuirass. It's the Royals, or the Enniskillens, or the Household. You can hear their cymbals and kettles. The French heavies are too good for us. They have ten to our one, and good men too. You've got to shoot at their faces or else at their horses. Mind you that when you see them coming, or else you'll find a four-foot sword stuck through your liver to teach you better. Hark! Hark! Hark!

126

There's the old music again!'

And as he spoke there came the low grumbling of a cannonade away somewhere to the east of us, deep and hoarse, like the roar of some blood-daubed beast that thrives on the lives of men. At the same instant there was a shouting of 'Heh! heh! heh!' from behind, and somebody roared, 'Let the guns get through!' Looking back, I saw the rear companies split suddenly in two and hurl themselves down on either side into the ditch, while six cream-coloured horses, galloping two and two with their bellies to the ground, came thundering through the gap with a fine twelve-pound gun whirling and creaking behind them. Behind were another, and another, four-and-twenty in all, flying past us with such a din and clatter, the blue-coated men clinging on to the gun and the tumbrils, the drivers cursing and cracking their whips, the manes flying, the mops and buckets clanking, and the whole air filled with the heavy rumble and the jingling of chains. There was a roar from the ditches, and a shout from the gunners, and we saw a rolling grey cloud before us, with a score of busbies breaking through the shadow. Then we closed up again, while the growling ahead of us grew louder and deeper than ever.

'There's three batteries there,' said the

sergeant. 'There's Bull's and Webber Smith's, but the other is new. There's some more on ahead of us, for here is the track of a nine-pounder, and the others were all twelves. Choose a twelve if you want to get hit; for a nine mashes you up, but a twelve snaps you like a carrot.' And then he went on to tell about the dreadful wounds that he had seen, until my blood ran like iced water in my veins, and you might have rubbed all our faces in pipeclay and we should have been no whiter. 'Aye, you'll look sicklier yet, when you get a hatful of grape into your tripes,' said he.

And then, as I saw some of the old soldiers laughing, I began to understand that this man was trying to frighten us; so I began to laugh also, and the others as well, but it was not a very hearty laugh either.

The sun was almost above us when we stopped at a little place called Hal, where there is an old pump from which I drew and drank a shako full of water — and never did a mug of Scotch ale taste as sweet. More guns passed us here, and Vivian's Hussars, three regiments of them, smart men with bonny brown horses, a treat to the eye. The noise of the cannons was louder than ever now, and it tingled through my nerves just as it had done years before, when, with Edie by my side, I had seen the merchant-ship fight with the privateers. It was so loud now that it seemed to me that the battle must be going on just beyond the nearest wood, but my friend the sergeant knew better.

'It's twelve to fifteen mile off,' said he. 'You may be sure the general knows we are not wanted, or we should not be resting here at Hal.'

What he said proved to be true, for a minute later down came the colonel with orders that we should pile arms and bivouac where we were; and there we stayed all day, while horse and foot and guns, English, Dutch, and Hanoverians, were streaming through. The devil's music went on till evening, sometimes rising into a roar, sometimes sinking into a grumble, until about eight o'clock in the evening it stopped altogether. We were eating our hearts out, as you may think, to know what it all meant, but we knew that what the Duke did would be for the best, so we just waited in patience.

Next day the brigade remained at Hal in the morning, but about mid-day came an orderly from the Duke, and we pushed on once more until we came to a little village called Braine something, and there we stopped; and time too, for a sudden thunderstorm broke over us, and a plump of rain that turned all the roads and the fields into bog and mire. We got into the barns at this village for shelter, and there we found two stragglers — one from a kilted regiment, and the other a man of the German Legion, who had a tale to tell that was as dreary as the weather.

Boney had thrashed the Prussians the day before, and our fellows had been sore put to it to hold their own against Ney, but had beaten him off at last. It seems an old stale story to you now, but you cannot think how we scrambled round those two men in the barn, and pushed and fought, just to catch a word of what they said, and how those who had heard were in turn mobbed by those who had not. We laughed and cheered and groaned all in turn as we heard how the 44th had received cavalry in line, how the Dutch-Belgians had fled, and how the Black Watch had taken the Lancers into their square, and then had killed them at their leisure. But the Lancers had had the laugh on their side when they crumpled up the 69th and carried off one of the colours. To wind it all up, the Duke was in retreat in order to keep in touch with the Prussians, and it was rumoured that he would take up his ground and fight a big battle just at the very place where we had been halted.

And soon we saw that this rumour was true; for the weather cleared towards evening, and we were all out on the ridge to see what we could see. It was such a bonny stretch of corn and grazing land, with the crops just half green and half yellow, and fine rye as high as a man's shoulder. A scene more full of peace you could not think of, and look where you would over the low curving corn-covered hills, you could see the little village steeples pricking up their spires among the poplars. But slashed right across this pretty picture was a long trail of marching men — some red, some green, some blue, some black — zigzagging over the plain and choking the roads, one end so close that we could shout to them, as they stacked their muskets on the ridge at our left, and the other end lost among the woods as far as we could see. And then on other roads we saw the teams of horses toiling and the dull gleam of the guns, and the men straining and swaying as they helped to turn the spokes in the deep, deep mud. As we stood there, regiment after regiment and brigade after brigade took position on the ridge, and ere the sun had set we lay in a line of over sixty thousand men, blocking Napoleon's way to Brussels. But the rain had come swishing down again, and we of the 71st rushed off to our barn once more, where we had better quarters than the greater part of our comrades, who lay stretched in the mud with the storm beating upon them until the first peep of day.

131

12

The Shadow on the Land

It was still drizzling in the morning, with brown drifting clouds and a damp chilly wind. It was a queer thing for me as I opened my eyes to think that I should be in a battle that day, though none of us ever thought it would be such a one as it proved to be. We were up and ready, however, with the first light, and as we threw open the doors of our barn we heard the most lovely music that I had ever listened to playing somewhere in the distance. We all stood in clusters hearkening to it, it was so sweet and innocent and sad-like. But our sergeant laughed when he saw how it pleased us all.

'Them are the French bands,' said he; 'and if you come out here you'll see what some of you may not live to see again.'

Out we went, the beautiful music still sounding in our ears, and stood on a rise just outside the barn. Down below at the bottom of the slope, about half a musket-shot from us, was a snug tiled farm with a hedge and a bit of an apple orchard. All round it a line of men in red coats and high fur hats were working like bees, knocking holes in the wall and barring up the doors.

'Them's the light companies of the Guards,' said the sergeant. 'They'll hold that farm while one of them can wag a finger. But look over yonder and you'll see the camp fires of the French.'

We looked across the valley at the low ridge upon the further side, and saw a thousand little yellow points of flame with the dark smoke wreathing up in the heavy air. There was another farm-house on the further side of the valley, and as we looked we suddenly saw a little group of horsemen appear on a knoll beside it and stare across at us. There were a dozen Hussars behind, and in front five men, three with helmets, one with a long straight red feather in his hat, and the last with a low cap.

'By God!' cried the sergeant, 'that's him! That's Boney, the one with the grey horse. Aye, I'll lay a month's pay on it.'

I strained my eyes to see him, this man who had cast that great shadow over Europe, which darkened the nations for five-and-twenty years, and which had even fallen across our out-of-the-world little sheep-farm, and had dragged us all — myself, Edie, and Jim — out of the lives that our folk had lived before us. As far as I could see, he was a dumpy square-shouldered kind of man, and he held his double glasses to his eyes with his elbows spread very wide out on each side. I was still staring when I heard the catch of a man's breath by my side, and there was Jim with his eyes glowing like two coals, and his face thrust over my shoulder.

'That's he, Jock,' he whispered.

'Yes, that's Boney,' said I.

'No, no, it's he. This de Lapp or de Lissac, or whatever his devil's name is. It is he.'

Then I saw him at once. It was the horseman with the high red feather in his hat. Even at that distance I could have sworn to the slope of his shoulders and the way he carried his head. I clapped my hands upon Jim's sleeve, for I could see that his blood was boiling at the sight of the man, and that he was ready for any madness. But at that moment Bonaparte seemed to lean over and say something to de Lissac, and the party wheeled and dashed away, while there came the bang of a gun and a white spray of smoke from a battery along the ridge. At the same instant the assembly was blown in our village, and we rushed for our arms and fell in. There was a burst of firing all along the line, and we thought that the battle had begun; but it came really from our fellows cleaning their pieces, for their priming was in some danger of being wet from the damp night.

From where we stood it was a sight now that was worth coming over the seas to see. On our own ridge was the chequer of red and blue stretching right away to a village over two miles from us. It was whispered from man to man in the ranks, however, that there was too much of the blue and too little of the red; for the Belgians had shown on the day before that their hearts were too soft for the work, and we had twenty thousand of them for comrades. Then, even our British troops were half made up of militiamen and recruits; for the pick of the old Peninsular regiments were on the ocean in transports, coming back from some fool's quarrel with our kinsfolk of America. But for all that we could see the bearskins of the Guards, two strong brigades of them, and the bonnets of the Highlanders, and the blue of the old German Legion, and the red lines of Pack's brigade, and Kempt's brigade and the green dotted riflemen in front, and we knew that come what might these were men who would bide where they were placed, and that they had a man to lead them who would place them where they should bide.

Of the French we had seen little save the twinkle of their fires, and a few horsemen here and there upon the curves of the ridge; but as we stood and waited there came suddenly a grand blare from their bands, and their whole army came flooding over the low hill which had hid them, brigade after brigade and division after division, until the broad slope in its whole length and depth was blue with their uniforms and bright with the glint of their weapons. It seemed that they would never have done, still pouring over and pouring over, while our men leaned on their muskets and smoked their pipes looking down at this grand gathering and listening to what the old soldiers who had fought the French before had to say about them. Then when the infantry had formed in long deep masses their guns came whirling and bounding down the slope, and it was pretty to see how smartly they unlimbered and were ready for action. And then at a stately trot down came the cavalry, thirty regiments at the least, with plume and breastplate, twinkling sword and fluttering lance, forming up at the flanks and rear, in long shifting, glimmering lines.

'Them's the chaps!' cried our old sergeant. 'They're gluttons to fight, they are. And you see them regiments with the great high hats in the middle, a bit behind the farm? That's the Guard, twenty thousand of them, my sons, and all picked men — grey-headed devils that have done nothing but fight since they were as high as my gaiters. They've three men to our two, and two guns to our one, and, by God! they'll make you recruities wish you were back in Argyle Street before they have finished with you.'

He was not a cheering man, our sergeant; but then he had been in every fight since Corunna, and had a medal with seven clasps upon his breast, so that he had a right to talk in his own fashion.

When the Frenchmen had all arranged themselves just out of cannon-shot we saw a small group of horsemen, all in a blaze with silver and scarlet and gold, ride swiftly between the divisions, and as they went a roar of cheering burst out from either side of them, and we could see arms outstretched to them and hands waving. An instant later the noise had died away, and the two armies stood facing each other in absolute deadly silence — a sight which often comes back to me in my dreams. Then, of a sudden, there was a lurch among the men just in front of us; a thin column wheeled off from the dense blue clump, and came swinging up towards the farm-house which lay below us. It had not taken fifty paces before a gun banged out from an English battery on our left, and the battle of Waterloo had begun.

It is not for me to try to tell you the story of that battle, and, indeed, I should have kept far enough away from such a thing had it not happened that our own fates, those of the three simple folk who came from the border country, were all just as much mixed up in it as those of any king or emperor of them all. To tell the honest truth, I have learned more about that battle from what I have read than from what I saw, for how much could I see with a comrade on either side, and a great white cloud-bank at the very end of my firelock? It was from books and the talk of others that I learned how the heavy cavalry charged, how they rode over the famous cuirassiers, and how they were cut to pieces before they could get back. From them, too, I learned all about the successive assaults, and how the Belgians fled, and how Pack and Kempt stood firm. But of my own knowledge I can only speak of what we saw during that long day in the rifts of the smoke and the lulls of the firing, and it is just of that that I will tell you.

We were on the right of the line and in reserve, for the Duke was afraid that Boney might work round on that side and get at him from behind; so our three regiments, with another British brigade and the Hanoverians, were placed there to be ready for anything.

There were two brigades of light cavalry, too; but the French attack was all from the front, so it was late in the day before we were really wanted.

The English battery which fired the first gun was still banging away on our left, and a German one was hard at work upon our right, so that we were wrapped round with the smoke; but we were not so hidden as to screen us from a line of French guns opposite, for a score of round shot came piping through the air and plumped right into the heart of us. As I heard the scream of them past my ear my head went down like a diver, but our sergeant gave me a prod in the back with the handle of his halbert.

'Don't be so blasted polite,' said he; 'when you're hit, you can bow once and for all.'

There was one of those balls that knocked five men into a bloody mash, and I saw it lying on the ground afterwards like a crimson football. Another went through the adjutant's horse with a plop like a stone in the mud, broke its back and left it lying like a burst gooseberry. Three more fell further to the right, and by the stir and cries we could tell that they had all told.

'Ah! James, you've lost a good mount,' says Major Reed, just in front of me, looking down at the adjutant, whose boots and breeches were all running with blood.

'I gave a cool fifty for him in Glasgow,' said the other. 'Don't you think, major, that the men had better lie down now that the guns have got our range?'

'Tut!' said the other; 'they are young, James, and it will do them good.'

'They'll get enough of it before the day's done,' grumbled the other; but at that moment Colonel Reynell saw that the Rifles and the 52nd were down on either side of us, so we had the order to stretch ourselves out too. Precious glad we were when we could hear the shot whining like hungry dogs within a few feet of our backs. Even now a thud and a splash every minute or so, with a yelp of pain and a drumming of boots upon the ground, told us that we were still losing heavily.

A thin rain was falling and the damp air held the smoke low, so that we could only catch glimpses of what was doing just in front of us, though the roar of the guns told us that the battle was general all along the lines. Four hundred of them were all crashing at once now, and the noise was enough to split the drum of your ear. Indeed, there was not one of us but had a singing in his head for many a long day afterwards. Just opposite us on the slope of the hill was a French gun, and we could see the men serving her quite plainly.

They were small active men, with very tight breeches and high hats with great straight plumes sticking up from them; but they worked like sheep-shearers, ramming and sponging and training. There were fourteen when I saw them first, and only four left standing at the last, but they were working away just as hard as ever.

The farm that they called Hougoumont was down in front of us, and all the morning we could see that a terrible fight was going on there, for the walls and the windows and the orchard hedges were all flame and smoke, and there rose such shrieking and crying from it as I never heard before. It was half burned down, and shattered with balls, and ten thousand men were hammering at the gates; but four hundred guardsmen held it in the morning and two hundred held it in the evening, and no French foot was ever set within its threshold. But how they fought, those Frenchmen! Their lives were no more to them than the mud under their feet. There was one — I can see him now — a stoutish ruddy man on a crutch. He hobbled up alone in a lull of the firing to the side gate of Hougoumont and he beat upon it, screaming to his men to come after him. For five minutes he stood there, strolling about in front of the gun-barrels which spared him, but at last a Brunswick skirmisher in the orchard flicked out his brains with a rifle shot. And he was only one of many, for all day when they did not come in masses they came in twos and threes with as brave a face as if the whole army were at their heels.

So we lay all morning, looking down at the fight at Hougoumont; but soon the Duke saw that there was nothing to fear upon his right, and so he began to use us in another way.

The French had pushed their skirmishers past the farm, and they lay among the young corn in front of us popping at the gunners, so that three pieces out of six on our left were lying with their men strewed in the mud all round them. But the Duke had his eyes everywhere, and up he galloped at that moment — a thin, dark, wiry man with very bright eyes, a hooked nose, and big cockade on his cap. There were a dozen officers at his heels, all as merry as if it were a foxhunt, but of the dozen there was not one left in the evening.

'Warm work, Adams,' said he as he rode up.

'Very warm, your grace,' said our general.

'But we can outstay them at it, I think. Tut, tut, we cannot let skirmishers silence a battery! Just drive those fellows out of that, Adams.'

Then first I knew what a devil's thrill runs through a man when he is given a bit of fighting to do. Up to now we had just lain and been killed, which is the weariest kind of work. Now it was our turn, and, my word, we were ready for it. Up we jumped, the whole brigade, in a four-deep line, and rushed at the cornfield as hard as we could tear. The skirmishers snapped at us as we came, and then away they bolted like corncrakes, their heads down, their backs rounded, and their muskets at the trail. Half of them got away; but we caught up the others, the officer first, for he was a very fat man who could not run fast. It gave me quite a turn when I saw Rob Stewart, on my right, stick his bayonet into the man's broad back and heard him howl like a damned soul. There was no quarter in that field, and it was butt or point for all of them. The men's blood was aflame, and little wonder, for these wasps had been stinging all morning without our being able so much as to see them.

And now, as we broke through the further edge of the cornfield, we got in front of the smoke, and there was the whole French army in position before us, with only two meadows and a narrow lane between us. We set up a yell as we saw them, and away we should have gone slap at them if we had been left to ourselves; for silly young soldiers never think that harm can come to them until it is there in their midst. But the Duke had cantered his horse beside us as we advanced, and now he roared something to the general, and the officers all rode in front of our line holding out their arms for us to stop. There was a blowing of bugles, a pushing and a shoving, with the sergeants cursing and digging us with their halberts; and in less time than it takes me to write it, there was the brigade in three neat little squares, all bristling with bayonets and in echelon, as they call it, so that each could fire across the face of the other.

It was the saving of us, as even so young a soldier as I was could very easily see; and we had none too much time either. There was a low rolling hill on our right flank, and from behind this there came a sound like nothing on this earth so much as the beat of the waves on the Berwick coast when the wind blows from the east. The earth was all shaking with that dull roaring sound, and the air was full of it.

'Steady, 71st! for God's sake, steady!' shrieked the voice of our colonel behind us; but in front was nothing but the green gentle slope of the grassland, all mottled with daisies and dandelions.

And then suddenly over the curve we saw eight hundred brass helmets rise up, all in a moment, each with a long tag of horsehair flying from its crest; and then eight hundred fierce brown faces all pushed forward, and glaring out from between the ears of as many horses. There was an instant of gleaming breast-plates, waving swords, tossing manes, fierce red nostrils opening and shutting, and hoofs pawing the air before us; and then down came the line of muskets, and our bullets smacked up against their armour like the clatter of a hailstorm upon a window. I fired with the rest, and then rammed down another charge as fast as I could, staring out through the smoke in front of me, where I could see some long, thin thing which napped slowly back-wards and forwards. A bugle sounded for us to cease firing, and a whiff of wind came to clear the curtain from in front of us, and then we could see what had happened.

I had expected to see half that regiment of horse lying on the ground; but whether it was that their breastplates had shielded them, or whether, being young and a little shaken at their coming, we had fired high, our volley had done no very great harm. About thirty horses lay about, three of them together within ten yards of me, the middle one right on its back with its four legs in the air, and it was one of these that I had seen flapping through the smoke. Then there were eight or ten dead men and about as many wounded, sitting dazed on the grass for the most part, though one was shouting 'Vive l'Empereur!' at the top of his voice. Another fellow who had been shot in the thigh — a great black-moustached chap he was too — leaned his back against his dead horse and, picking up his carbine, fired as coolly as if he had been shooting for a prize, and hit Angus Myres, who was only two from me, right through the forehead. Then he out with his hand to get another carbine that lay near, but before he could reach it big Hodgson, who was the pivot man of the Grenadier company, ran out and passed his bayonet through his throat, which was a pity, for he seemed to be a very fine man.

At first I thought that the cuirassiers had run away in the smoke; but they were not men who did that very easily. Their horses had swerved at our volley, and they had raced past our square and taken the fire of the two other ones beyond. Then they broke through a hedge, and coming on a regiment of Hanoverians who were in line, they treated them as they would have treated us if we had not been so quick, and cut them to pieces in an instant. It was dreadful to see the big

Germans running and screaming while the cuirassiers stood up in their stirrups to have a better sweep for their long, heavy swords, and cut and stabbed without mercy. I do not believe that a hundred men of that regiment were left alive; and the Frenchmen came back across our front, shouting at us and waving their weapons, which were crimson down to the hilts. This they did to draw our fire, but the colonel was too old a soldier; for we could have done little harm at the distance, and they would have been among us before we could reload.

These horsemen got behind the ridge on our right again, and we knew very well that if we opened up from the squares they would be down upon us in a twinkle. On the other hand, it was hard to bide as we were; for they had passed the word to a battery of twelve guns, which formed up a few hundred yards away from us, but out of our sight, sending their balls just over the brow and down into the midst of us, which is called a plunging fire. And one of their gunners ran up on to the top of the slope and stuck a handspike into the wet earth to give them a guide, under the very muzzles of the whole brigade, none of whom fired a shot at him, each leaving him to the other. Ensign Samson, who was the youngest subaltern in the regiment, ran out from the square and pulled down the handspike; but quick as a jack after a minnow, a lancer came flying over the ridge, and he made such a thrust from behind that not only his point but his pennon too came out between the second and third buttons of the lad's tunic. 'Helen! Helen!' he shouted, and fell dead on his face, while the lancer, blown half to pieces with musket balls, toppled over beside him, still holding on to his weapon, so that they lay together with that dreadful bond still connecting them.

But when the battery opened there was no time for us to think of anything else. A square is a very good way of meeting a horseman, but there is no worse one of taking a cannon ball, as we soon learned when they began to cut red seams through us, until our ears were weary of the slosh and splash when hard iron met living flesh and blood. After ten minutes of it we moved our square a hundred paces to the right; but we left another square behind us, for a hundred and twenty men and seven officers showed where we had been standing. Then the guns found us out again, and we tried to open out into line; but in an instant the horsemen — lancers they were this time — were upon us from over the brae.

I tell you we were glad to hear the thud of their hoofs, for we knew that that must stop the cannon for a minute and give us a chance of hitting back. And we hit back pretty hard too that time, for we were cold and vicious and savage, and I for one felt that I cared no more for the horsemen than if they had been so many sheep on Corriemuir. One gets past being afraid or thinking of one's own skin after a while, and you just feel that you want to make some one pay for all you have gone through. We took our change out of the lancers that time; for they had no breastplates to shield them, and we cleared seventy of them out of their saddles at a volley. Maybe, if we could have seen seventy mothers weeping for their lads, we should not have felt so pleased over it; but then, men are just brutes when they are fighting, and have as much thought as two bull pups when they've got one another by the throttle.

Then the colonel did a wise stroke; for he reckoned that this would stave off the cavalry for five minutes, so he wheeled us into line, and got us back into a deeper hollow out of reach of the guns before they could open again. This gave us time to breathe, and we wanted it too, for the regiment had been melting away like an icicle in the sun. But bad as it was for us, it was a deal worse for some of the others. The whole of the Dutch Belgians were off by this time helter-skelter, fifteen thousand of them, and there were great gaps left in our line through which the French cavalry rode as pleased them best. Then the French guns had been too many and too good for ours, and our heavy horse had been cut to bits, so that things were none too merry with us. On the other hand, Hougoumont, a blood-soaked ruin, was still ours, and every British regiment was firm; though, to tell the honest truth, as a man is bound to do, there were a sprinkling of red coats among the blue ones who made for the rear. But these were lads and stragglers, the faint hearts that are found everywhere, and I say again that no regiment flinched. It was little we could see of the battle; but a man would be blind not to know that all the fields behind us were covered with flying men. But then, though we on the right wing knew nothing of it, the Prussians had begun to show, and Napoleon had set 20,000 of his men to face them, which made up for ours that had bolted, and left us much as we began. That was all dark to us, however; and there was a time, when the French horsemen had flooded in between us and the rest of the army, that we thought we were the only brigade left standing, and had set our teeth with the intention of selling our lives as dearly as we could.

At that time it was between four and five in the afternoon, and we had had nothing to eat, the most of us, since the night before, and were soaked with rain into the bargain. It had drizzled off and on all day, but for the last few hours we had not had a thought to spare either upon the weather or our hunger. Now we began to look round and tighten our waist-belts, and ask who was hit and who was spared. I was glad to see Jim, with his face all blackened with powder, standing on my right rear, leaning on his firelock. He saw me looking at him, and shouted out to know if I were hurt.

'All right, Jim,' I answered.

'I fear I'm here on a wild-goose chase,' said he gloomily, 'but it's not over yet. By God, I'll have him, or he'll have me!'

He had brooded so much on his wrong, had poor Jim, that I really believe that it had turned his head; for he had a glare in his eyes as he spoke that was hardly human. He was always a man that took even a little thing to heart, and since Edie had left him I am sure that he was no longer his own master.

It was at this time of the fight that we saw two single fights, which they tell me were common enough in the battles of old, before men were trained in masses. As we lay in the hollow two horsemen came spurring along

151

the ridge right in front of us, riding as hard as hoof could rattle. The first was an English dragoon, his face right down on his horse's mane, with a French cuirassier, an old, grey-headed fellow, thundering behind him, on a big black mare. Our chaps set up a hooting as they came flying on, for it seemed shame to see an Englishman run like that; but as they swept across our front we saw where the trouble lay. The dragoon had dropped his sword, and was unarmed, while the other was pressing him so close that he could not get a weapon. At last, stung maybe by our hooting, he made up his mind to chance it. His eye fell on a lance beside a dead Frenchman, so he swerved his horse to let the other pass, and hopping off cleverly enough, he gripped hold of it. But the other was too tricky for him, and was on him like a shot. The dragoon thrust up with the lance, but the other turned it, and sliced him through the shoulder-blade. It was all done in an instant, and the Frenchman cantering his horse up the brae, showing his teeth at us over his shoulder like a snarling dog.

That was one to them, but we scored one for us presently. They had pushed forward a skirmish line, whose fire was towards the batteries on our right and left rather than on us; but we sent out two companies of the

95th to keep them in check. It was strange to hear the crackling kind of noise that they made, for both sides were using the rifle. An officer stood among the French skirmishers — a tall, lean man with a mantle over his shoulders — and as our fellows came forward he ran out midway between the two parties and stood as a fencer would, with his sword up and his head back. I can see him now, with his lowered eyelids and the kind of sneer that he had upon his face. On this the subaltern of the Rifles, who was a fine well-grown lad, ran forward and drove full tilt at him with one of the queer crooked swords that the rifle-men carry. They came together like two rams — for each ran for the other — and down they tumbled at the shock, but the Frenchman was below. Our man broke his sword short off, and took the other's blade through his left arm; but he was the stronger man, and he managed to let the life out of his enemy with the jagged stump of his blade. I thought that the French skirmishers would have shot him down, but not a trigger was drawn, and he got back to his company with one sword through his arm and half of another in his hand.

13

The End of the Storm

Of all the things that seem strange in that battle, now that I look back upon it, there is nothing that was queerer than the way in which it acted on my comrades; for some took it as though it had been their daily meat without question or change, and others pattered out prayers from the first gunfire to the last, and others again cursed and swore in a way that was creepy to listen to. There was one, my own left-hand man, Mike Threadingham, who kept telling about his maiden aunt, Sarah, and how she had left the money which had been promised to him to a home for the children of drowned sailors. Again and again he told me this story, and yet when the battle was over he took his oath that he had never opened his lips all day. As to me, I cannot say whether I spoke or not, but I know that my mind and my memory were clearer than I can ever remember them, and I was thinking all the time about the old folk at home, and about Cousin Edie with her saucy, dancing eyes, and de Lissac with his cat's whiskers, and all the doings at West Inch, which had ended by bringing us here on the plains of Belgium as a cockshot for two hundred and fifty cannons.

During all this time the roaring of those guns had been something dreadful to listen to, but now they suddenly died away, though it was like the lull in a thunderstorm when one feels that a worse crash is coming hard at the fringe of it. There was still a mighty noise on the distant wing, where the Prussians were pushing their way onwards, but that was two miles away. The other batteries, both French and English, were silent, and the smoke cleared so that the armies could see a little of each other. It was a dreary sight along our ridge, for there seemed to be just a few scattered knots of red and the lines of green where the German Legion stood, while the masses of the French appeared to be as thick as ever, though of course we knew that they must have lost many thousands in these attacks. We heard a great cheering and shouting from among them, and then suddenly all their batteries opened together with a roar which made the din of the earlier part seem nothing in comparison. It might well be twice as loud, for every battery was twice as near, being moved right up to point blank range, with huge masses of horse between and behind them to guard them from attack.

When that devil's roar burst upon our ears there was not a man, down to the drummer boys, who did not understand what it meant. It was Napoleon's last great effort to crush us. There were but two more hours of light, and if we could hold our own for those all would be well. Starved and weary and spent, we prayed that we might have strength to load and stab and fire while one of us stood upon his feet.

His cannon could do us no great hurt now, for we were on our faces, and in an instant we could turn into a huddle of bayonets if his horse came down again. But behind the thunder of the guns there rose a sharper, shriller noise, whirring and rattling, the wildest, jauntiest, most stirring kind of sound.

'It's the *pas-de-charge!*' cried an officer. 'They mean business this time!'

And as he spoke we saw a strange thing. A Frenchman, dressed as an officer of hussars, came galloping towards us on a little bay horse. He was screeching '*Vive le roi! Vive le roi!*' at the pitch of his lungs, which was as much as to say that he was a deserter, since we were for the king and they for the emperor. As he passed us he roared out in English, 'The Guard is coming! The Guard is coming!' and so vanished away to the rear like a leaf blown before a storm. At the same instant up there rode an aide-de-camp, with the reddest face that ever I saw upon mortal man.

'You must stop 'em, or we are done!' he cried to General Adams, so that all our company could hear him.

'How is it going?' asked the general.

'Two weak squadrons left out of six regiments of heavies,' said he, and began to laugh like a man whose nerves are overstrung.

'Perhaps you would care to join in our advance? Pray consider yourself quite one of us,' said the general, bowing and smiling as if he were asking him to a dish of tea.

'I shall have much pleasure,' said the other, taking off his hat; and a moment afterwards our three regiments closed up, and the brigade advanced in four lines over the hollow where we had lain in square, and out beyond to the point whence we had seen the French army.

There was little of it to be seen now, only the red belching of the guns flashing quickly out of the cloudbank, and the black figures — stooping, straining, mopping, sponging — working like devils, and at devilish work. But through the cloud that rattle and whirr rose ever louder and louder, with a deep-mouthed shouting and the stamping of thousands of feet. Then there came a broad black blur through the haze, which darkened and hardened until we could see that it was a hundred men abreast, marching swiftly towards us, with high fur hats upon their heads and a gleam of brasswork over their brows. And behind that hundred came another hundred, and behind that another, and on and on, coiling and writhing out of the cannon-smoke like a monstrous snake, until there seemed to be no end to the mighty column. In front ran a spray of skirmishers, and behind them the drummers, and up they all came together at a kind of tripping step, with the officers clustering thickly at the sides and waving their swords and cheering. There were a dozen mounted men too at their front, all shouting together, and one with his hat held aloft upon his swordpoint. I say again, that no men upon this earth could have fought more manfully than the French did upon that day.

It was wonderful to see them; for as they came onwards they got ahead of their own guns, so that they had no longer any help from them, while they got in front of the two batteries which had been on either side of us all day. Every gun had their range to a foot, and we saw long red lines scored right down the dark column as it advanced. So near were they, and so closely did they march, that every shot ploughed through ten files of them, and yet they closed up and came on with a swing and dash that was fine to see. Their head was turned straight for ourselves, while the 95th overlapped them on one side and the 52nd on the other.

I shall always think that if we had waited so the Guard would have broken us; for how could a four-deep line stand against such a column? But at that moment Colburne, the colonel of the 52nd, swung his right flank round so as to bring it on the side of the column, which brought the Frenchmen to a halt. Their front line was forty paces from us at the moment, and we had a good look at them. It was funny to me to remember that I had always thought of Frenchmen as small men; for there was not one of that first company who could not have picked me up as if I had been a child, and their great hats made them look taller yet. They were hard, wizened, wiry fellows too, with fierce puckered eyes and bristling moustaches, old soldiers who had fought and fought, week in, week out, for many a year. And then, as I stood with my finger upon the trigger waiting for the word to fire, my eye fell full upon the mounted officer with his hat upon his sword, and I saw that it was de Lissac.

I saw it, and Jim did too. I heard a shout, and saw him rush forward madly at the

French column; and, as quick as thought, the whole brigade took their cue from him, officers and all, and flung themselves upon the Guard in front, while our comrades charged them on the flanks. We had been waiting for the order, and they all thought now that it had been given; but you may take my word for it, that Jim Horscroft was the real leader of the brigade when we charged the Old Guard.

God knows what happened during that mad five minutes. I remember putting my musket against a blue coat and pulling the trigger, and that the man could not fall because he was so wedged in the crowd; but I saw a horrid blotch upon the cloth, and a thin curl of smoke from it as if it had taken fire. Then I found myself thrown up against two big Frenchmen, and so squeezed together, the three of us, that we could not raise a weapon. One of them, a fellow with a very large nose, got his hand up to my throat, and I felt that I was a chicken in his grasp. 'Rendez-vous, coqin; rendez-vous!' said he, and then suddenly doubled up with a scream, for someone had stabbed him in the bowels with a bayonet. There was very little firing after the first sputter; but there was the crash of butt against barrel, the short cries of stricken men, and the roaring of the officers.

And then, suddenly, they began to give ground — slowly, sullenly, step by step, but still to give ground. Ah! it was worth all that we had gone through, the thrill of that moment, when we felt that they were going to break. There was one Frenchman before me, a sharp-faced, dark-eyed man, who was loading and firing as quietly as if he were at practice, dwelling upon his aim, and looking round first to try and pick off an officer. I remember that it struck me that to kill so cool a man as that would be a good service, and I rushed at him and drove my bayonet into him. He turned as I struck him and fired full into my face, and the bullet left a weal across my cheek which will mark me to my dying day. I tripped over him as he fell, and two others tumbling over me I was half smothered in the heap. When at last I struggled out, and cleared my eyes, which were half full of powder, I saw that the column had fairly broken, and was shredding into groups of men, who were either running for their lives or were fighting back to back in a vain attempt to check the brigade, which was still sweeping onwards. My face felt as if a red-hot iron had been laid across it; but I had the use of my limbs, so jumping over the litter of dead and mangled men, I scampered after my regiment, and fell in upon the right flank.

Old Major Elliott was there, limping along, for his horse had been shot, but none the worse in himself. He saw me come up, and nodded, but it was too busy a time for words. The brigade was still advancing, but the general rode in front of me with his chin upon his shoulder, looking back at the British position.

'There is no general advance,' said he; 'but I'm not going back.'

'The Duke of Wellington has won a great victory,' cried the aide-de-camp, in a solemn voice; and then, his feelings getting the better of him, he added, 'if the damned fool would only push on!' — which set us all laughing in the flank company.

But now anyone could see that the French army was breaking up. The columns and squadrons which had stood so squarely all day were now all ragged at the edges; and where there had been thick fringes of skirmishers in front, there were now a spray of stragglers in the rear. The Guard thinned out in front of us as we pushed on, and we found twelve guns looking us in the face, but we were over them in a moment; and I saw our youngest subaltern, next to him who had been killed by the lancer, scribbling great 71's with a lump of chalk upon them, like the schoolboy that he was. It was at that moment that we heard a roar of cheering behind us, and saw the whole British army flood over the crest of the ridge, and come pouring down upon the remains of their enemies. The guns, too, came bounding and rattling forward, and our light cavalry — as much as was left of it — kept pace with our brigade upon the right. There was no battle after that. The advance went on without a check, until our army stood lined upon the very ground which the French had held in the morning. Their guns were ours, their foot were a rabble spread over the face of the country, and their gallant cavalry alone was able to preserve some sort of order and to draw off unbroken from the field. Then at last, just as the night began to gather, our weary and starving men were able to let the Prussians take the job over, and to pile their arms upon the ground that they had won. That was as much as I saw or can tell you about the Battle of Waterloo, except that I ate a two-pound rye loaf for my supper that night, with as much salt meat as they would let me have, and a good pitcher of red wine, until I had to bore a new hole at the end of my belt, and then it fitted me as tight as a hoop to a barrel. After that I lay down in the straw where the rest of the company were sprawling, and in less than a minute I was in a dead sleep.

14

The Tally of Death

Day was breaking, and the first grey light had just begun to steal through the long thin slits in the walls of our barn, when someone shook me hard by the shoulder, and up I jumped. I had the thought in my stupid, sleepy brain that the cuirassiers were upon us, and I gripped hold of a halbert that was leaning against the wall; but then, as I saw the long lines of sleepers, I remembered where I was. But I can tell you that I stared when I saw that it was none other than Major Elliott that had roused me up. His face was very grave, and behind him stood two sergeants, with long slips of paper and pencils in their hands.

'Wake up, laddie,' said the Major, quite in his old easy fashion, as if we were back on Corriemuir again.

'Yes, Major?' I stammered.

'I want you to come with me. I feel that I owe something to you two lads, for it was I that took you from your homes. Jim Horscroft is missing.'

I gave a start at that, for what with the rush

and the hunger and the weariness I had never given a thought to my friend since the time that he had rushed at the French Guards with the whole regiment at his heels.

'I am going out now to take a tally of our losses,' said the Major; 'and if you cared to come with me, I should be very glad to have you.'

So off we set, the Major, the two sergeants, and I; and oh! but it was a dreadful, dreadful sight! — so much so, that even now, after so many years, I had rather say as little of it as possible. It was bad to see in the heat of fight; but now in the cold morning, with no cheer or drum-tap or bugle blare, all the glory had gone out of it, and it was just one huge butcher's shop, where poor devils had been ripped and burst and smashed, as though we had tried to make a mock of God's image. There on the ground one could read every stage of yesterday's fight — the dead footmen that lay in squares and the fringe of dead horsemen that had charged them, and above on the slope the dead gunners, who lay round their broken piece. The Guards' column had left a streak right up the field like the trail of a snail, and at the head of it the blue coats were lying heaped upon the red ones where that fierce tug had been before they took their backward step.

And the very first thing that I saw when I got there was Jim himself. He was lying on the broad of his back, his face turned up towards the sky, and all the passion and the trouble seemed to have passed clean away from him, so that he looked just like the old Jim as I had seen him in his cot a hundred times when we were schoolmates together. I had given a cry of grief at the sight of him; but when I came to look upon his face, and to see how much happier he looked in death than I could ever have hoped to see him in life, it was hard to mourn for him. Two French bayonets had passed through his chest, and he had died in an instant, and without pain, if one could believe the smile upon his lips.

The Major and I were raising his head in the hope that some flutter of life might remain, when I heard a well-remembered voice at my side, and there was de Lissac leaning upon his elbow among a litter of dead guardsmen. He had a great blue coat muffled round him, and the hat with the high red plume was lying on the ground beside him. He was very pale, and had dark blotches under his eyes, but otherwise he was as he had ever been, with the keen, hungry nose, the wiry moustache, and the close-cropped head thinning away to baldness upon the top.

His eyelids had always drooped, but now one could hardly see the glint of his eyes from beneath them.

'Hola, Jock!' he cried. 'I didn't thought to have seen you here, and yet I might have known it, too, when I saw friend Jim.'

'It is you that has brought all this trouble,' said I.

'Ta, ta, ta!' he cried, in his old impatient fashion. 'It is all arranged for us. When I was in Spain I learned to believe in Fate. It is Fate which has sent you here this morning.'

'This man's blood lies at your door,' said I, with my hand on poor Jim's shoulder.

'And mine on his, so we have paid our debts.'

He flung open his mantle as he spoke, and I saw with horror that a great black lump of clotted blood was hanging out of his side.

'This is my thirteenth and last,' said he, with a smile. 'They say that thirteen is an unlucky number. Could you spare me a drink from your flask?'

The Major had some brandy and water. De Lissac supped it up eagerly. His eyes brightened, and a little fleck of colour came back in each of his haggard cheeks.

'It was Jim did this,' said he. 'I heard someone calling my name, and there he was with his gun against my tunic. Two of my men cut him down just as he fired. Well, well, Edie was worth it all! You will be in Paris in less than a month, Jock, and you will see her. You will find her at No. 11 of the Rue Miromesnil, which is near to the Madeleine. Break it very gently to her, Jock, for you cannot think how she loved me. Tell her that all I have are in the two black trunks, and that Antoine has the keys. You will not forget?'

'I will remember.'

'And madame, your mother? I trust that you have left her very well. And monsieur, too, your father? Bear them my distinguished regards!'

Even now as death closed in upon him, he gave the old bow and wave as he sent his greetings to my mother.

'Surely,' said I, 'your wound may not be so serious as you think. I could bring the surgeon of our regiment to you.'

'My dear Jock, I have not been giving and taking wounds this fifteen years without knowing when one has come home. But it is as well, for I know that all is ended for my little man, and I had rather go with my Voltigeurs than remain to be an exile and a beggar. Besides, it is quite certain that the Allies would have shot me, so I have saved myself from that humiliation.'

'The Allies, sir,' said the Major, with some

heat, 'would be guilty of no such barbarous action.'

But de Lissac shook his head, with the same sad smile.

'You do not know, Major,' said he. 'Do you suppose that I should have fled to Scotland and changed my name if I had not more to fear than my comrades who remained in Paris? I was anxious to live, for I was sure that my little man would come back. Now I had rather die, for he will never lead an army again. But I have done things that could not be forgiven. It was I that led the party which took and shot the Due d'Enghien. It was I — Ah, *mon Dieu! Edie, Edie, ma cherie!*'

He threw out both his hands, with all the fingers feeling and quivering in the air. Then he let them drop heavily in front of him, and his chin fell forward upon his chest. One of our sergeants laid him gently down, and the other stretched the big blue mantle over him; and so we left those two whom Fate had so strangely brought together, the Scotchman and the Frenchman, lying silently and peacefully within hand's touch of each other, upon the blood-soaked hillside near Hougoumont.

15

The End of It

And now I have very nearly come to the end of it all, and precious glad I shall be to find myself there; for I began this old memory with a light heart, thinking that it would give me some work for the long summer evenings, but as I went on I wakened a thousand sleeping sorrows and half-forgotten griefs, and now my soul is all as raw as the hide of an ill-sheared sheep. If I come safely out of it I will swear never to set pen to paper again, for it is so easy at first, like walking into a shelving stream, and then before you can look round you are off your feet and down in a hole, and can struggle out as best you may.

We buried Jim and de Lissac with four hundred and thirty-one others of the French Guards and our own Light Infantry in a single trench. Ah! if you could sow a brave man as you sow a seed, there should be a fine crop of heroes coming up there some day! Then we left that bloody battle-field behind us for ever, and with our brigade we marched on over the French border on our way to Paris.

I had always been brought up during all these years to look upon the French as very evil folk, and as we only heard of them in connection with fightings and slaughterings, by land and by sea, it was natural enough to think that they were vicious by nature and ill to meet with. But then, after all, they had only heard of us in the same fashion, and so, no doubt, they had just the same idea of us. But when we came to go through their country, and to see their bonny little steadings, and the douce quiet folk at work in the fields, and the women knitting by the road-side, and the old granny with a big white mutch smacking the baby to teach it manners, it was all so home-like that I could not think why it was that we had been hating and fearing these good people for so long. But I suppose that in truth it was really the man who was over them that we hated, and now that he was gone and his great shadow cleared from the land, all was brightness once more.

We jogged along happily enough through the loveliest country that ever I set my eyes on, until we came to the great city, where we thought that maybe there would be a battle, for there are so many folk in it that if only one in twenty comes out it would make a fine army. But by that time they had seen that it was a pity to spoil the whole country just for the sake of one man, and so they had told him that he must shift for himself in the future. The next we heard was that he had surrendered to the British, and that the gates of Paris were opened to us, which was very good news to me, for I could get along very well just on the one battle that I had had.

But there were plenty of folk in Paris now who loved Boney; and that was natural when you think of the glory that he had brought them, and how he had never asked his army to go where he would not go himself. They had stern enough faces for us, I can tell you, when we marched in, and we of Adams' brigade were the very first who set foot in the city. We passed over a bridge which they call Neuilly, which is easier to write than to say, and through a fine park — the Bois de Boulogne, and so into the Champs d'Elysees. There we bivouacked, and pretty soon the streets were so full of Prussians and English that it became more like a camp than a city.

The very first time that I could get away I went with Rob Stewart, of my company — for we were only allowed to go about in couples — to the Rue Miromesnil. Rob waited in the hall, and I was shown upstairs; and as I put my foot over the mat, there was Cousin Edie, just the same as ever, staring at me with those wild eyes of hers. For a moment she did not recognise me, but when she did she just took three steps forward and sprang at me, with her two arms round my neck.

'Oh, my dear old Jock,' she cried, 'how fine you look in a red coat!'

'Yes, I am a soldier now, Edie,' said I, very stiffly; for as I looked at her pretty face, I seemed to see behind it that other face which had looked up to the morning sky on the Belgium battle-field.

'Fancy that!' she cried. 'What are you, then, Jock? A general? A captain?'

'No, I am a private.'

'What! Not one of the common people who carry guns?'

'Yes, I carry a gun.'

'Oh, that is not nearly so interesting,' said she. And she went back to the sofa from which she had risen. It was a wonderful room, all silk and velvet and shiny things, and I felt inclined to go back to give my boots another rub. As Edie sat down again, I saw that she was all in black, and so I knew that she had heard of de Lissac's death.

'I am glad to see that you know all,' said I, for I am a clumsy hand at breaking things. 'He said that you were to keep whatever was in the boxes, and that Antoine had the keys.'

'Thank you, Jock, thank you,' said she. 'It

was like your kindness to bring the message. I heard of it nearly a week ago. I was mad for the time — quite mad. I shall wear mourning all my days, although you can see what a fright it makes me look. Ah! I shall never get over it. I shall take the veil and die in a convent.'

'If you please, madame,' said a maid, looking in, 'the Count de Beton wishes to see you.'

'My dear Jock,' said Edie, jumping up, 'this is very important. I am sorry to cut our chat short, but I am sure that you will come to see me again, will you not, when I am less desolate? And would you mind going out by the side door instead of the main one? Thank you, you dear old Jock; you were always such a good boy, and did exactly what you were told.'

And that was the last that I was ever to see of Cousin Edie. She stood in the sunlight with the old challenge in her eyes, and flash of her teeth; and so I shall always remember her, shining and unstable, like a drop of quicksilver. As I joined my comrade in the street below, I saw a grand carriage and pair at the door, and I knew that she had asked me to slip out so that her grand new friends might never know what common people she had been associated with in her childhood.

She had never asked for Jim, nor for my father and mother who had been so kind to her. Well, it was just her way, and she could no more help it than a rabbit can help wagging its scut, and yet it made me heavy-hearted to think of it. Two months later I heard that she had married this same Count de Beton, and she died in child-bed a year or two later.

And as for us, our work was done, for the great shadow had been cleared away from Europe, and should no longer be thrown across the breadth of the lands, over peaceful farms and little villages, darkening the lives which should have been so happy. I came back to Corriemuir after I had bought my discharge, and there, when my father died, I took over the sheep-farm, and married Lucy Deane, of Berwick, and have brought up seven children, who are all taller than their father, and take mighty good care that he shall not forget it. But in the quiet, peaceful days that pass now, each as like the other as so many Scotch tups, I can hardly get the young folks to believe that even here we have had our romance, when Jim and I went a-wooing, and the man with the cat's whiskers came up from the sea.

We do hope that you have enjoyed reading this large print book.

Did you know that all of our titles are available for purchase?

We publish a wide range of high quality large print books including:
Romances, Mysteries, Classics
General Fiction
Non Fiction and Westerns

Special interest titles available in large print are:
The Little Oxford Dictionary
Music Book
Song Book
Hymn Book
Service Book

Also available from us courtesy of Oxford University Press:
Young Readers' Dictionary
(large print edition)
Young Readers' Thesaurus
(large print edition)

For further information or a free brochure, please contact us at:
Ulverscroft Large Print Books Ltd.,
The Green, Bradgate Road, Anstey,
Leicester, LE7 7FU, England.
Tel: (00 44) 0116 236 4325
Fax: (00 44) 0116 234 0205

DUBLINERS

James Joyce

1890s Ireland: Across the city of Dublin, as the River Liffey winds and twinkles through its heart, infinite domestic dramas play themselves out behind lace curtains and broken window-panes, inside quiet parlours and crammed churches, along concrete pavements and cinder paths. Through these are illuminated snippets of the lives of the Dubliners — truants, seducers, gossips, rally-drivers, generous hostesses, corrupt politicians, failing priests, amateur theologians, struggling musicians, moony adolescents, victims of domestic brutishness, sentimental aunts and poets, patriots earnest or cynical . . . and people just striving to get by.

OLD FRIENDS AND NEW FANCIES

Sybil G. Brinton

When Georgiana Darcy and Colonel Robert Fitzwilliam break off their engagement, confessing that their mutual affection remains purely platonic, each is free to seek their spouse elsewhere. After seeing her perform in a concert, Robert warms to the beautiful and talented Mary Crawford — but Lady Catherine de Bourgh pays heed to spiteful tongues, and drives Mary from Rosings. Meanwhile, Kitty Bennet is staying in London as the protégée of a certain young lady named Emma Knightley. When introduced to charming naval officer William Price, younger brother of Fanny, Kitty swiftly loses her heart to him. But when William and Georgiana meet, will Kitty's dreams be shattered?